Sair Back, Sair Banes

Anthony Engebretson

Sair Back, Sair Banes

First published in Great Britain 2022 by Ghost Orchid Press

ISBN (e-book): 978-1-7399968-3-3

ISBN (paperback): 978-1-7399968-2-6

Cover photograph © andreiuc88 via. Shutterstock

Book formatting and cover design by Claire Saag

To Nama, one of my first fans and critics

CHAPTER ONE

It was like a painting—a generic, inoffensive, and pretty landscape portrait. The kind you would see in a hotel room or a dentist's office. The loch—its choppy grey waters reflecting the cloud-covered sky, light wisps of mist along its surface—surrounded by massive green hills blanketed by trees. It was, for all intents and purposes, haunting, magical, and breathtaking. At least it was supposed to be. But even though she was right there, close enough to touch the water, the cool wind kissing her face and filling her nostrils with a dewy smell, Genevieve felt like she was staring at a painting, nothing more.

She tried to let herself be enveloped by its majesty—awakened to the beauty this sight offered her. To bask in every sensation. She was finally *here*, after all. Scotland. Her dream trip since she was little.

But all she felt was tired. Cold, too, despite her three layers. The damned wind was sending chills through her body and her hair was getting in her face. Not to mention her back was killing her, as usual. When had she become so brittle?

A morning walk had seemed like a pleasant idea. But now, she just wanted to hike back to Janet's house and crawl into bed. Funny, she was never one for sleeping in. Of course, she had never been one for taking vacations either.

Okay.

She closed her eyes and took a deep breath. Inhale for five counts, exhale for ten: a grounding technique she'd learned from one, or maybe all, of her therapists. It never worked but always seemed worth a try. Once she sucked in and blew out as much as possible and opened her eyes, she had the sudden feeling that she wasn't alone.

There was nobody around, as far as she could tell. The only other signs of life were the whistling of birds and two boats out on the water—speckled dots floating along the distant shore. She looked behind her, where up the hill perched Janet's house and the rest of the village. There was hardly a soul except for two lone figures: a man and his dog walking along the trail. The only sounds, aside from the birds, were the wind beating against her eardrums, and water sloshing at the shore.

She was alone.

But for some reason, the feeling of being watched pressed all around her. No, not just watched; *leered* at. When she looked back at the loch, the water seemed darker than before, inviting her with a cold and violating gaze.

It was definitely time to go back.

She strode up the hill, her heart racing, as if the loch itself was inching after her.

But before she could get too far, new noises erupted behind her; the desperate sounds of splashing, snorting and grunting. They came abruptly, as if someone had turned on a radio. Despite her instincts to keep moving, she paused and looked back at the loch. A dark shape now stood in those choppy dark waters. A horse. A black one, large as she'd ever seen, with a mane that poured down its neck. It was breast deep in the water, not far from where she had been standing. Where the hell had it come from? Maybe it had been nearby all this time, and she just hadn't noticed it. Regardless, it seemed stuck. It was thrashing its head about, snorting, grunting, occasionally squealing, its eyes white with terror. The poor thing was probably stuck in some mud or seaweed.

"Hey!" she shouted, hoping someone—anyone who wasn't her—would hear. But there was no answer—even the man and his dog seemed to have disappeared. The little town of Fonniskie wasn't awake yet.

Her mind spinning, she slowly stepped toward the shore where the horse continued its pathetic thrashing. She futilely called out a couple more times. But she knew nobody could help the creature but her. An urge told her to run back up to the village and wake someone up. Maybe that would be best; she didn't know what to do. Even if she had the gumption to jump into the water, she had no idea how to calm a horse and guide it back to shore. She'd always hated horses—though not enough to let one drown, apparently.

For the first time in a long time, or maybe ever, she wished Todd were with her. He was no equine expert either, as far as she knew. But he would have at least pigheadedly dove in there, would have tried to do *something*.

The horse continued its fruitless struggling.

"Give me a moment," she said. Unsurprisingly, these words did nothing to calm the frightened animal. But perhaps she had said it more to herself. Every step brought her closer toward the water. She still didn't know what she would do once she could step no further on dry land.

The horse's thrashing became more violent and desperate, splashing water onto her legs. It threw its head to the sky, large teeth bared as it squealed. Its cries vibrated through her ears.

"Please," she whispered, slowly reaching her trembling hand out.

Though she wasn't yet close enough to touch it, the horse suddenly stopped its struggling and looked at her. Its eyes still had that frightened look, and it snorted and bristled, but it had gone from eleven to three with an abruptness that baffled Genevieve. As it gazed at her, the cold and oppressive feeling she'd had earlier crept back in. But this time, she didn't feel she could retreat. She felt trapped, boxed in by this creature's stare. All she could do was take another step, her fingertips stretching toward the horse's mane. The creature itself seemed to be leaning in, its eyes narrowing. Genevieve didn't know what she was doing or what she was planning to do next. All that mattered was getting closer. Soon, she smelled nothing but the horse—a warm, musky stench—and she could feel a dampness emanating from the animal, coating her own skin.

Just get a little closer.

A high-pitched bark jolted her out of this trance. She jerked her hand away as the horse raised its head and let out a furious squeal. Genevieve turned to see the source of the barking: a rutty, black and white collie dog. It was snarling aggressively, not at her, but at the horse. The dog's owner, a stocky man with a long

white beard, was lumbering after, shouting and curs-
ing.

When she looked back to the water, her heart
skipped a beat, and her throat went dry. The horse was
gone. There was barely even a ripple where it had been.
It was as if the loch had swiftly and silently sucked it
in.

CHAPTER TWO

"I hope this is fine."

"Oh, it looks perfect. Thank you."

Janet Duncan shuffled into the seat across from Genevieve. "Well, I haven't cooked a traditional breakfast like this in quite a while. Usually, it's just porridge and tea for me."

Genevieve gave a blank smile. Truthfully, this was far more than she could eat: fried eggs, square sausages, toast, baked beans, and berries. Her "breakfasts" were usually a cup of coffee and maybe some pretzels or dark chocolate. Besides, she didn't have much of an appetite after basically witnessing an animal drown.

Of course, she wasn't fully sure that was what had happened. When the man with the dog had reached her, profusely apologizing for his "barking menace," she had asked him if he'd seen the horse.

"A horse? Cannae say I did. Of course, my eyes aren't what they used to be."

He had stayed with her a while, helping her scan the water for some sign of the animal. But the search had come to nothing. The horse must have sunk like a stone. Or maybe it just swam off somewhere.

Perhaps it hadn't been there at all. Yet she hoped it had. This was the worst time and place for her to start hallucinating.

Genevieve picked a raspberry from her cup and downed it like a pill, hoping it would kick her appetite in. She wasn't about to insult Janet by eschewing this feast.

The little old woman's face wrinkled in a warm smile. "It's so good to see you, dear," she said. Her soft voice and lilting accent trickled through Genevieve's ears like honey.

"It's good to see you, too."

"Last time I saw you ... "

"It was quite a while ago." Genevieve popped another raspberry.

"Aye, you were just a girl. Now look at you, a beautiful grown woman."

Genevieve put on another smile. Janet had said the same thing the night before. But their meeting had been short, as Genevieve had arrived late, just around Janet's bedtime. Now they were catching up properly.

The old woman began reminiscing about the time she had visited America and stayed with Genevieve's family. Genevieve personally didn't care for reminiscing, but she listened politely, nibbling on her food. Janet seemed to remember that time—over thirty years ago—much more thoroughly than she did. Genevieve had been in high school, back when everyone called her "Gen". All she remembered was barely being home enough to spend much time with her family, let alone with the visiting Janet Duncan. Between studying, track, being in FBLA, she'd had too much on her plate. So many things that had seemed so very important.

At one point in the reminiscing, Janet's smile faded. "I'm so sorry I couldn't make it to your mother's funeral."

"Oh ... " It was strange to hear it said aloud: "your mother's funeral", even though it was nearly a year since. Sometimes, it still felt like Genevieve could give her a "quick" call. A call that her mother would extend with updates about her friends and comments about the events of the day. In all honesty, she hadn't felt much grief, at least not as much as she should have. It wasn't that she didn't miss her mother, but that death hadn't hit her the way her Dad's had. Perhaps it was simply because her mother had died peacefully, at an age when it seemed okay to die.

"I would have come if I could," Janet said.

"Oh, it's okay."

"No." There was a tremble in Janet's voice. "It broke my heart enough to miss your Da's funeral."

Genevieve had a sudden image of her father lying lifelessly on his bed, skin pale and mouth frothing, an empty bottle of pills on his nightstand. She had never actually seen that scene—it had been her mother who'd found him. But it was an image that haunted her, even after so long. She mentally pushed the thought away, along with the memory of his funeral. That day had felt like the end of the world. She hadn't stepped foot in a church since. Her mother's funeral had mercifully been held entirely at the cemetery.

"She was a good woman," Janet said, dabbing her moist eyes with a napkin. "She did not have to keep writing or calling after your Da died. But I'm happy she did." She balled up the napkin and chuckled. "Look at me, sitting here greetin' all over the table when all you want to do is eat your breakfast."

"It's okay." Genevieve tore off a bird's portion of toast.

Janet frowned at Genevieve's barely touched plate. "Is it all right?"

"Uh, yes." Genevieve's stomach dropped; the last thing she wanted to do was offend her host. "It just—" she decided to let a little honesty seep in. "Usually, it takes time for my appetite to wake up, you know?"

"Oh, of course." Janet grimaced, the distress on her face touchingly genuine. "I should have asked before I made all this!"

Genevieve considered reaching across the table and touching Janet's hand, but decided not to. "It's okay, I really do appreciate it." To demonstrate, she ate a small sliver of egg.

"I was just so excited to have you here. Didn't think twice about it. I suppose porridge will do tomorrow then?"

Genevieve nodded and took a sip of tea; she could at least finish that.

Janet ate a couple bites in silence. "It's a little much for me, too," she said, sighing remorsefully. Then, in a sudden instant, her small blue eyes lit up and she chuckled. "I remember when your Da was here. He would eat everything Ma gave him. Would suck it up like a vacuum and still have room for seconds. You'd think he hadn't eaten for days!"

Genevieve put on a smile and nodded. She tried to picture her dad here, in this very kitchen, over sixty years ago. A sprightly young man with his whole life ahead of him, leaving a "victory plate" after every meal. How much had this kitchen changed since then? Surely the appliances were new? The washing machine in the corner looked the oldest, but even that couldn't have been more than fifteen years old. But the checkerboard floors, the yellowing white cupboards, the rustic wooden table, walls cluttered with darkened pots and pans, that sweet yet bitter smell in the air—had all those things been here, that summer long ago? Did he take walks down to the loch as she had? What would he have done had he seen that horse in distress? Would he have just stood there?

"Any plans for today then?" Janet asked, snapping Genevieve from her thoughts.

"Um. No, not really." She took a courtesy nibble out of one of the sausages.

"You should drop by the Wet Hoof sometime. I'm sure Mara would love to meet you."

"The Wet Hoof?"

"Aye, the pub."

A pub sounded like the last place Genevieve would want to go, but she politely nodded. "I don't know where that is."

"Oh, you can't miss it. It's by the river. You know, that house used to be in my family. My uncle lived there when I was a lass. When he died, my parents moved there and left me *this* house. I suppose they'd hoped I would take up a husband and start a family of my own. Well ... " She smiled and shrugged, sipping her tea. "When they died, I didn't know what to do with the place, so I sold it to a woman from Glesga ... Glasgow. Mara. Wonderful woman. A little strange, mind. Some folks might think her a bit of a crabbit, at first. You remind me a bit of her."

That gave Genevieve pause. Was she a "crabbit", whatever that meant? She tried to come across as pleasant as possible. Acceptable, at the very least.

"I remember when I first met her," Janet continued with a dreamy look in her eyes. "I'd never met a woman more beautiful. She can have a very icy and direct way about her—all business. But when you get to know her ... " She chuckled to herself before slowly dropping from her dewy-eyed trance and grinning at Genevieve. "Well, I had my doubts about her turning the old house into a pub. But she's done quite a bit of good with it. I've only been a few times myself, mind. But it always seems to be the place to be."

"I'll have to check it out," Genevieve said, trying to sound convincing but not committed.

"Well, do tell Mara hello. It's been too long since I've had the chance to speak with her."

Their partially eaten breakfasts grew cold as the conversation went on. Janet needled Genevieve, asking for updates on her brothers, her nieces, her nephew. Good, good, all doing well. Then the woman told more stories about Genevieve's father—the crass jokes he would tell, many Genevieve herself could remember vividly; the time he taught Janet to swim; the time he nearly drowned in the loch.

"What?" This last anecdote snapped Genevieve from her complacent daze.

"Aye, thankfully Da was there to dive in and drag him out. It was a strange thing. The way Da described it, the loch just seemed to pull Allen in and didn't want to give him back. Allen didn't swim the rest of the summer."

"He never told me that." Perhaps her dad had felt no reason to. Whatever anxiety he had developed about bodies of water had eventually subsided. Throughout her childhood, he took her and her brothers to lakes all the time. So much of her summers had been filled with boating, swimming, and fishing. In fact, he had always dreamed of buying a house by a lake, with a private dock of his own. It was Genevieve who hated the water—the one who had always preferred to stay in the boat, who never went tubing or water skiing, who only swam as close to the beach as she could, if she swam at all.

Janet went on to tell various stories about the village—when Mrs. So-and-so's cat went missing and nearly the whole town tried to help find it, only to discover it had been hiding in her crawlspace all along; when the such-and-such family's house burned down in a freak accident and everybody pitched in to build them a new one; when this happened, and that happened, and laughs and tears were had by all.

It was near lunchtime when breakfast finally ended. When the dishes were put away, Genevieve wandered back upstairs to the guest bedroom to read. She rested on top of the massive bed, a quilt pulled up to her knees, and a book in her hands. It was the first book in a historical romance series that she thought she'd try. She hadn't read a fiction book since ... maybe college.

By the time she reached the fourth page, she realized she couldn't pay attention to the text and gave up. Her back was screaming, no matter how much ibuprofen she took. This was one of those days where she wished she would allow herself to take stronger pain-killers. But no, it wasn't worth the risk. What if she spiraled into addiction? And if it ended up killing her, who would find her body? Maybe one of her brothers, but it would take a few months for them to worry about not hearing from her. More likely her landlord, when rent was long due—and by then she would be rotted in her bed or wherever she happened to drop.

No, Advil would have to do. Once she got home, she would schedule an appointment with her chiropractor. The treatments always seemed to help, for a time.

She laid herself flat, closed her eyes, and tried to meditate. After a couple of minutes, she sat up again and did what she'd promised herself she wouldn't do, grabbing her laptop to check her emails. She imagined her team had been excited to not hear from her for a couple of weeks. Too bad. It didn't hurt to make sure they were doing everything right. She was the head of marketing at an architectural firm, one of the largest in Omaha. Though she'd been in that position for nineteen years, her superiors—some of whom had been with the company for a quarter as long—thought they knew her job better. After an hour of reading, drafting, and sending emails, her back's angry protests became impossible to ignore, and she laid flat again.

It was hard to pinpoint when her back problems had started. She suspected it had happened during a boating trip in Iowa. Her then-husband, Todd, had bought a cheap old motorboat, perhaps thinking it would help save their marriage. Fittingly, the boat had sputtered and died in the middle of the lake. While Todd had insisted on fixing the motor, Genevieve had just wanted to get to shore. She'd strained herself with paddling until her husband had finally thrown away his pride and helped. Yet another reason for her to hate the water.

She sighed deeply, staring at the ceiling. Here she was—the first and perhaps only international trip of her life—in the little village she used to dream about, lying in bed, reading emails, and reflecting on her disastrous life.

Honestly, why the hell was she in Fonniskie? Why did she decide to spend five days here? She didn't want to go out to the loch; she hardly even wanted to look at it after this morning. She couldn't even say she was keeping a lonely old woman company. Janet was out visiting a neighbor, and after that she was going to help another neighbor with his gardening. That woman had more friends than she knew what to do with. At least in Glasgow and Edinburgh Genevieve had taken some tours. Sure, Fonniskie was always meant to be the

"R&R" portion of the trip. But she had never planned what "R&R" would even mean. If only she'd taken up a hobby.

She closed her eyes, then gently drifted into a brief snooze. She dreamt she was riding a horse—a large black horse—galloping through a landscape that could have been anywhere between the Scottish Highlands and the Nebraska farmlands. The horse was swiftly carrying her toward a lake. She tried to steer it in another direction, but it wouldn't respond. She couldn't get off its back either. They were moving too fast and, well, she seemed to be stuck to it.

As the horse leapt into the water, she jerked awake.

It had been a strange variation of those brief "falling" dreams she would have from time to time. It was clear where this one came from: the horse, the loch. Though there was something else just below the surface. Thinking about the dream gave her dark, uneasy feelings. Feelings she'd only ever felt as a small child.

Her stomach gurgled, bringing her back to the present. She sat up, her back pain seeming to have eased off a bit. It was time to get out of bed and scrounge some lunch.

Janet had told her she was free to help herself to anything she wanted. She wasn't too comfortable digging through someone else's kitchen. After briefly searching the creaky old cupboard, she decided a bowl of Cheerios and some berries would be fine.

As she ate her lunch—her mind numbly silent—she looked out the window. The sky was blue, and the sun was shining white and bright. For whatever reason, it stirred something in her, an old urge she thought had long faded with "Gen." The urge to go out there, to explore, to take a chance.

Genevieve kept close to the village, avoiding the loch. There appeared to be more activity on the water now: boating, fishing, swimming. It was much warmer than it had been in the morning, and the ever-present wind had died down some. Her layers felt a bit much now.

It was strange to be walking through Fonniskie—a village she'd heard and thought about throughout her life. Now, being here, it just felt like any random old town.

Certainly, there were things that made it different from towns back home. The streets were narrower, with far fewer cars. The houses seemed older. Everything was so clean, too, she hardly came across any litter, and the air smelled fresh, if a bit salty. The village was also somehow quieter than anywhere else she'd ever been. The townspeople were incredibly warm and friendly. Not just the "Midwest Nice" veneer of politeness—one she herself had mastered—where people smiled at you through their teeth as long as you didn't cause a stir. Maybe the denizens of Fonniskie were just better at faking it, she thought. One woman even stopped to say hello and talk about the weather, as if Genevieve was a local herself. She nervously fumbled through the conversation before quickly moving on.

Yet despite these differences, a part of her felt like she could just get into a car, pop off onto I-80 and drive a few miles to her stuffy little apartment.

It took twenty minutes or so to walk the entire town. As far as she knew, the population was around 150, though that didn't account for the tourists who came and went. There was a community center, a little cafe converted from the old post office, a small hotel, a few guest houses, a "mom-and-pop" grocery, and little else. This was the kind of quaint town she used to imagine living in, raising a family. Of course, she'd grown out of that fantasy; she grew content with her home city, settled into a cushy job, and realized she didn't even want kids. If there was one thing about her marriage that had been right, it was that Todd hadn't wanted any either.

Toward the end of her excursion, she strolled along the small river that fed into the loch. It looked crisp and clear—not muddy like the rivers back home. She remembered hearing that Fonniskie was derived from the Scottish Gaelic word for "Underwater." Perhaps the town had been hit by a flood at some point.

This thought conjured the image of that black horse, struggling in the water. It made her feel sick with guilt.

Again, she asked herself what she could have done, and couldn't come up with a better answer besides "more".

Near where the river melded into the loch was a large stone house. It had a small gravel parking lot near its entrance. In front of the lot was a blue sign in the shape of a hoof print: "The Wet Hoof". So, this was the pub Janet had mentioned. It didn't appear to be open yet, and Genevieve still couldn't imagine being interested in going there once it did. Though the idea seemed less repellant than it had earlier.

The afternoon warmth caught up to her, and Genevieve was practically panting. Stopping to take off her damp jacket, she noticed a lone figure in the parking lot. A thin woman in a white dress, standing near the river's edge, stared out at the gentle water. There was something captivating about the woman. It could have been her upright and alert posture or her statuesque stillness. Or maybe it was the dense silver hair that flowed all the way to her slender hips. The woman slowly craned her head toward Genevieve, her face long and pale. Her piercing copper-colored eyes stared daggers at Genevieve. Embarrassed and a little panicked, Genevieve quickly looked away and continued walking.

The blue, triangular little house where Janet lived was just a block from the pub. Genevieve was too swampy and fatigued to continue her walk, and her back quivered with pain. Still, she wasn't sure what she would do with the rest of her time. She gazed across the road from the house, down the hill where the loch awaited. Despite the blotches of human activity along its surface, it seemed still, the water shimmering brightly in the sun.

A tight feeling pressed into her. That feeling again, of being gawked at by hungry, slobbering eyes. She charged back into the house, almost locking the front door behind her. She decided not to, though Janet would have been able to let herself in; when heading out, the woman had taken her house key, attached to a bedazzling white and blue lanyard.

Once inside, the oppressive feeling slowly subsided. Genevieve sighed and let her nerves settle.

A shower. A cold shower would be good. Those never failed to relax her, and it would make her feel less gross.

Besides, it would be something productive to do.

CHAPTER THREE

Janet whipped up another big meal for dinner: Bangers and Mash.

"Ma's old recipe. Your father used to love it, so I thought you should try it. I hope it turned out all right."

This time, Genevieve was truly hungry, practically shoveling down the rich sausages and mashed potatoes. All the while Janet reminisced about her childhood, her parents, Genevieve's father. Genevieve hardly had to say a thing as the older woman never tired of talking. Through it all, her voice remained soft and cheery, her face wrinkled with smiles. Genevieve had no idea how someone could be so happy—or at least act so happy. But there was a warmth about the woman she couldn't help but bask in.

Even before arriving, she had felt comfortable with Janet. When she had emailed Janet out of the blue, stating her plans to visit Fonniskie, the woman had sent her back a wordy, excited email about how it had been so long, how she was thrilled, how Genevieve would stay at her house, and she wouldn't hear any arguments about it.

By the meal's end, both plates were only half finished, but Genevieve's stomach was completely full.

"Any plans for this evening?" Janet asked, wiping her mouth.

"Oh." Genevieve pictured going back to her room, maybe trying to read her book again before going to sleep. But it was only about 7:15—or 19:15 as Janet's oven clock said—the sun hadn't even set yet, and she was wide awake. "I don't know. What are your plans?"

Janet laughed. "Truth be told, I'm knackered. I'll probably be heading to bed early tonight. I'm sorry I can't keep you company. You're welcome to the television if you like. I have a few puzzles around, too. Or, if you're wanting to get out of the house, the Wet Hoof's open."

The pub. No chance of that ...

Well, maybe it would be fun. She could at least drop in for a short bit, just to say that she did. She never cared for the bar scene, but maybe a genuine Scottish pub would be different. What else would she do, lie on the couch and watch TV until she could barely lift her eyes? Well, that didn't seem too bad. But tonight ...

Maybe she could just pop in for a minute or two.

The place smelled of alcohol and musk, but it was clean. The tables, floors and seats practically sparkled. It had a cozy feeling to it—the lights low and orange, the walls a rustic brown adorned with fading old photographs and posters. It was quiet, too; no music, which Genevieve was grateful for. The loudest sound was the persistent and bombastic laughter of two men in a corner. They were about the only patrons so far. Aside from them and Genevieve was an old man hunched at the bar. Behind the bar was a younger man who greeted Genevieve with a big, squirrely smile.

"Hello there," he said.

"Hello," Genevieve said, sitting along the bar and not fully making eye contact with the bartender.

"American, then?" he asked. "Or maybe Canadian?"

Genevieve wondered if it would be wise to honestly answer that. But the man's light and chipper tone, enhanced by his soft accent, seemed friendly enough.

"American."

"Ah, excellent. We're happy to have you here."

Someone stepped out from a room behind the bar, carrying a large box. Genevieve's heart stopped as she recognized the silver-haired woman. It was the woman she had seen staring out at the river earlier. The woman's copper eyes turned toward Genevieve for a brief moment before shifting back to the task at hand.

"What'll it be then?" The bartender asked Genevieve, his lanky body hovering awkwardly over the bar.

"Oh, um ... " She didn't even feel like a drink. Would it have been insulting to just ask for a still water or something? Her dad always used to tell her that

Scots were proud of their whiskey, so she decided to ask for a scotch whiskey on the rocks.

"Any particular brand?"

She shrugged. "Surprise me."

The bartender smiled wide and turned to fix her drink. She realized she should have asked for something cheap. But it was too late, and it didn't really matter anyway.

"So, what brings you to our wee town?" The bartender asked as he slid her a tumbler of The Famous Grouse. "I'm Gordon, by the way."

"Hi. Genevieve. I'm just visiting."

Gordon opened his mouth but was interrupted.

"You're Janet's guest, are you not?" The asker had a firm, steely voice that seemed to fill the room. It was the silver-haired woman, whose eyes were fixed on Genevieve, commanding her to answer.

"Yes."

"Janet Duncan?" said Gordon. "Oh, aye! How do you know her?"

"She's an old family friend," Genevieve said, looking into her whiskey.

"Huh, I never knew Janet had American friends."

"Your father lived with her family for a time," the silver-haired woman again interjected. "Am I correct?"

"A summer, correct." She was stunned by how the woman would know that. At the same time, it surely it was no great mystery how word traveled fast in a town like this. "He studied abroad at Edinburgh for a year. Back in college."

"Edinburgh!" Gordon squeaked excitedly. "I'm from there! Do you know where he studied?"

"I don't, sorry."

"Gordon," the silver-haired woman affectionately patted his shoulder, "let the poor woman drink in peace."

Gordon raised his hands in concession. "You're right, you're right. I'm sorry."

Time went on, and other patrons began to wander in. Some were tourists, cautiously bumbling their way inside like Genevieve had. Others were locals who greeted Gordon by name. They also greeted the silver-haired woman—Mara. So *that* was Mara, the owner of the pub that Janet had spoken so fondly of. Mara must've been older than she appeared, then—she only looked fifty, at most.

As the room filled up, Genevieve began feeling suffocated. A sea of people surrounded her, chatting, laughing, embracing the friendship and warmth of another; and here she was, the mushy, flavorless grape in an otherwise vibrant fruit cocktail. Though her drink was only half finished, she decided it was time to leave.

"So can I ask you something?" Gordon said, just as she began wiggling from her seat. "What brought your father here? To Fonniskie?"

"I, uh, I don't really know." She leaned back, hoping to indicate that she was about to leave.

"Well," Gordon didn't seem to pick up on the body language, "maybe he fell in love. With the town, I mean. Or the loch. I certainly did."

"Yes, maybe." In truth, she knew why her dad had chosen to spend that summer in Fonniskie. According to him, his great-grandparents had lived in the village before packing up and leaving for America. Whether that was true or not, Genevieve didn't know. But if the town hadn't been a part of her family before her dad's summer there, it certainly was since.

Gordon looked like he was ready to ask another question and she interrupted him with a loud click of the tongue. "Well, I think I ... "

"You ever find that horse?" came a voice beside her. It was the old man, a couple seats down—one of the people who had been here when she arrived. Seeing his face now, grinning through that long white beard, she recognized him—the man with the dog from that morning.

"No, I didn't."

"What's this about a horse, George?" Gordon asked.

"Oh, this morning the lass said she saw a horse drowning in the loch." Genevieve had to strain herself to understand George's thick accent. "Didnae see it meself."

"That's odd," Gordon frowned and looked thought-fully at the counter. "Who around here owns horses?"

George shrugged. "Must've come from out of town." He sipped his pint and chuckled. "Maybe it was a kelpie."

"A kelpie?" Gordon said. "Well, then I suppose we're in quite a bit of trouble then."

"Aye."

Kelpie. That sounded familiar. It made her think back to another time in life—those vulnerable, lonely, but wondrous years of childhood. Then she remembered. Her dad used to love telling her and her brothers scary stories, especially when they were all little. He reveled in telling them at any time and any place, whether it was around a campfire or in the car on the way to the store. Among these stories were those of the kelpies, water horses that inhabited lochs, rivers, seas. The creatures were mischievous, playful, and sometimes dangerous. Being shapeshifters, they would lure their prey in with mundane forms. Usually, a kelpie would take the form of a regular land horse. When its victim (often children, and especially those who happened to be around whatever ages Genevieve and her brothers were at the time) hopped onto the creature's back, they would become stuck to it, helpless as it dragged them into the water to drown. Along with piranhas, sharks, and parasites, they became another reason she hated lakes or any body of water that wasn't a public swimming pool—though those, too, were repellant for their own reasons.

"I don't think I've ever seen a horse in town," Gordon said, shrugging helplessly.

"I have," said George. "Saw one near the river once. A big grey mare."

Mara floated in from behind Gordon; Genevieve hadn't even noticed her back there. "Aye, you numpty," the woman said to George. "I'm sure you're a trusted eyewitness." She pointed at his glass. "Is that your fourth?"

"Third and a half," George responded, exchanging a playful smile with Mara.

"Do you know anyone around here who might own a horse?" Gordon asked her.

All the playfulness faded from Mara's eyes when she turned to Genevieve. "I'm sure she was just seeing things."

At first, she was in her office, with its windowless lighting and barely decorated walls. She rested her hands along her characteristically barren desk, waiting. Soon, she would be off on a big trip. But her parents were supposed to come say goodbye first. Time crawled by and they didn't show. She tried to call each of them, but only heard muffled, distant voices on the other line. Agitation overwhelmed her body, to the point where she began screaming at the top of her lungs, but no scream was satisfying enough.

Next thing she knew, she was bareback riding a massive coal-black horse. Her body was stuck to it, an unnecessary appendage wobbling along its back. It was hurtling toward a loch. Now, she couldn't even scream. All she could do was ride along helplessly. It wasn't over when they hit the dark water. She was dragged under the choppy water, still powerless to move, unable to breathe. Panic consumed her as she sank deeper and deeper. She was being taken. She was going to die.

Then, once there was nothing but the cold, suffocating darkness, Genevieve finally awoke, gasping. Apparently, she'd been sleeping face down in her pillow. That had never happened to her before. She usually slept on her back, especially since her pains started.

Rolling herself over like a pathetic, skinny turtle, she gazed up at the ceiling. There was hardly a sound except for the permanent rushing in her ears and the whistling and cracking of the wind against the house.

Her eyes became heavy but were pulled open again by a low thudding outside. The sound was slow but consistent, a heavy clopping. Hooves. Her breath stopped when she heard a low snort.

She couldn't have been hearing things correctly. Who would be riding a horse at this time of night?

Carefully, she pulled herself from bed, her back giving subtle pings of protest, and looked out the window. There wasn't any sign of life or movement in the moonlit world. It quickly became clear that the sound was gone as well, no matter how hard she listened for it. There was nothing here but her, the street, and the black expanse beyond, its true nature exposed by the moon's bright reflection along its waters.

The loch, still as it was, seemed to be as awake as her.

CHAPTER FOUR

Following a breakfast of thick porridge and berries, Janet went out to visit another neighbor. Genevieve felt a little saddened by the old woman's departure, as she didn't want to be left alone. Besides, in her short and strange time in Fonniskie, listening to the soft, dreamy reminiscences of an old family friend had been a comfort. Of course, Janet had invited her to come along. But in the end, it was better to be alone in a semi-stranger's house than having to socialize with a complete stranger.

She had no urge to walk today. Outside it was grey, cold, and drizzly; the stereotypical Scottish day Genevieve had always imagined. Instead, she brought her laptop down to the living room to work. The room didn't look like it had changed in at least fifty years. Other than the flat screen TV above the fireplace, everything seemed as if it had been there for a long time— the old stone fireplace, the lumpy green sofa and the wooden rocking chair next to it. There was a scuffed and scratched chest that made for a makeshift coffee table; she vaguely wondered what was inside. The walls were smothered by old black and white photos of Janet's parents, of Janet as a child and a teenager. On the fireplace mantle was a faded picture of Janet and Genevieve's father, ages twelve and twenty respectively, smiling in front of the loch.

Next to that was a photo of Genevieve's family. It must have been taken when Genevieve was around eight or nine. The grainy, over-exposed picture showed them all standing stiffly in front of the Grand Canyon, her parents with their outdated hairstyles and large sunglasses, the three kids in front of them, beaming and squinting in the sun. Genevieve didn't remember a thing about that trip. But the photo, to her own surprise, made her smile.

After a few moments of checking and composing emails, she was interrupted by a knock at the front door. She groaned at the prospect of answering it, but then remembered this was Janet's house, not hers. Whoever it was had come for Janet. She could ignore them. But the knock kept coming. There was a desperate cadence to it, loud and aggressive. Soon she began to hear a high, masculine voice, shouting indiscernible pleas. An urge told Genevieve to run upstairs, retreat into the bathroom until this person went away. Whatever their reason for being here, it was no concern of hers.

Time went on and the knocking and shouting didn't let up. Genevieve finally relented, pulling her tired body from the couch. She reminded herself that she was an adult, that she'd been handling people all her life and always did fine. What was the worst that could happen?

At first, upon opening the front door, she thought it was a mannequin standing before her in the drizzling rain. It appeared to be a young man, face pale and unnaturally smooth. The face was almost too perfect, from the small, straight nose to the full lips. Pale as he was, he had dark features. His symmetrical eyes were dark brown, and his rutty, long hair was black. He had a glazed, stage-frightened look and paid no heed to the rain drizzling down his hair, his face, his black raincoat.

"Can I help you?" Genevieve asked.

The pale man didn't snap from his daze. She began to wonder if there was something on her face. When she asked again, more firmly this time, he finally blinked and opened his mouth.

"Oh yes, my name is Murdock. I ... um ... I need help." There was something flat and robotic about his voice. A lingering hint of an accent was there; she didn't know if it was a form of Scottish or from some other part of the British Isles. Regardless, it sounded almost fabricated.

"Oh? Well, I don't know ... "

"My boat," Murdock pointed toward the loch. "It capsized."

Already, she regretted opening the door. "Well, maybe someone ... "

"My wife and sister are down there. They're hurt. Can you come with me?"

If what he was saying was true, she had a moral obligation to go with him. But something was off, wrong. She wished more than ever that Janet was here.

"Please," Murdock said. His tone was desperate but—it could've been the flat voice—it seemed empty.

"Okay," Genevieve said. "Let me get my jacket and we'll see if one of the neighbors can—"

"There isn't time." Murdock reached for her, and she instinctively jerked away. Startled by her reaction, he eased back. "My sister needs help."

"And your wife?"

Murdock stared blankly for a moment, and then blinked. "Yes, her too."

That did it, she wasn't going to go anywhere with this man, not alone. "Maybe we need to call the police."

"Please," said Murdock, pointing again to the loch. "It's just down the hill."

"I can't do anything."

Murdock's face was no longer blank. He had an angry glare, so intense it seemed the color faded from his eyes. Genevieve also realized that he stank, badly. The smell was musty, damp and animalistic—the stink of a flooded barn. She also noticed something in his hair, a dark green strand tangled among the black. It looked like seaweed.

"Maybe there's someone at the outdoor center," she said. That wasn't necessarily reasonable, as the center was on the other side of the loch, but if it got him as far from her as possible ...

"No," Murdock growled, stepping forward.

She jerked away. "Back off!"

Suddenly the anger faded from Murdock's face. He had the wide-eyed look of an animal that heard a sudden noise. He looked to the street, where a small, hunched figure in a coat was hobbling toward them. Genevieve breathed out with relief. Janet.

Murdock looked back to Genevieve, his lips pursing hesitantly. She pushed her fear away as best as she could and glared at him, putting on that steely look she'd developed when her marriage collapsed, a look she'd further honed to impress deadlines on her team. However, Murdock didn't seem intimidated at all, only ponderous. She breathed in deep, giving herself enough oxygen to shout as loudly as possible, knowing that at least Janet would hear.

Finally, Murdock frowned and nodded. "The outdoor center." Saying nothing else, he turned and ran, rounding the corner of the house and vanishing from sight.

Genevieve breathed out and trembled. She couldn't move, her brain couldn't even configure what had just happened.

"What's gotten into you, dear?" Janet asked, shuffling down the front walkway.

The elderly woman ushered Genevieve back inside, sitting her down on the living room couch and fixing them both some tea. When Genevieve finally composed herself, she told Janet all that had just happened.

"Oh dear," was all Janet said in response.

"You saw him, right?" Genevieve asked, her heart picking up.

"Aye, I saw him," Janet said. Genevieve could have cried with relief—at least she knew for sure *he* wasn't imagined. "I was wondering what had him in such a hurry. Poor thing was speeding down the road like a racehorse."

"Do you know who that was?"

Janet shook her head. "I can't say I'd ever seen him before. Probably from out of town." She stared into her tea and sighed. "How awful. Poor dears. I wish there was something I could do. But I'm sure they're getting the help they need."

Genevieve nodded, not mentioning the doubts and suspicions that flooded her mind.

After dinner, she decided to venture down to the Wet Hoof pub again. She hadn't thought she'd ever want to go back, but after her encounter this morning, she had an urge to be around people for a while.

Gordon greeted her warmly when she entered. Mara, less so. She remembered Janet describing Mara as a "crabbit", but it was more than that—the woman clearly didn't like her. At this point in her life, she thought she was unfazed by being disliked. But for whatever reason, Mara's underhanded resentment bothered her. George was also here again, but he only greeted her with a quick smile and nod before turning back to his drink.

Red wine sounded good; it wasn't something she'd had in a long time. After ordering a glass, she sat at a table in the corner. Quietly, she sat alone, watching as the place filled up. Her breath tightened each time the door opened, anticipating that the next person who entered would be Murdock. But it never was. As much as she wanted to, she couldn't get her strange encounter with him out of her head. Maybe she had been in the wrong, and Murdock had been telling the truth. His strange behavior could have just been a man dazed after such an accident. In that case, she was an awful person for refusing to help him and his injured wife and sister.

But if her doubts were right, if he *had* been lying ... Then she shuddered to imagine what his goal might have been.

There was something else, silly as it was: she couldn't help but think about kelpies again. There was an aspect of her dad's stories that had come back to her. Sometimes, the creatures would shapeshift into people. This human form would be beautiful and alluring to draw in human prey. Kelpies that lived in the lochs—sometimes they were called another name, some Gaelic word that Genevieve couldn't remember—especially loved to prey on young women and typically took the form of a handsome young man. But there were certain tells to help one know they were dealing with a kelpie. One was if they had hooves instead of feet. Another was seaweed in their hair.

She could have laughed at the icy chills running through her body. It was incredible how the human mind took stories and coincidences and tried to find a pattern in it.

But fairy tales or not, the gnawing fear and discomfort inside her was very real. It kept her glued to her

seat, staying much longer than she had last night—
watching customers come and go. Before she knew it,
the place was quiet, and she had two and a half empty
glasses in front of her. Even George had left, giving
another quick smile and nod in her direction before
heading out the door. According to her phone, it was
11:52 p.m., which explained why her body was beginning to feel like shutting down. But she was terrified at
the thought of walking back to Janet's house alone in
the dark. It probably had been a bad idea to go out tonight.

Gordon came to her table, a pint of beer in hand.
"Oh," she said, waving her hands, "I didn't order ... "

He took a sip, perhaps to demonstrate that it was his.
"Can I sit?" he said, pointing to the seat across from
her.

She wasn't in the mood for conversation, and the
last thing she needed was another young man creeping
on her. But at the same time, the room was nearly
empty of bodies, and she wasn't ready to be alone. Besides, she never got any alarm bells from Gordon. He
just seemed like an obnoxiously friendly guy. He

wasn't just congenial to her, either—between last night and tonight, she had never seen anyone tirelessly engage in lively conversation with so many people. She nodded.

"Thank you."

But then, something in her mind told her, *you've missed alarm bells before.*

"Genevieve, right?" he asked after settling into his seat.

"Yes."

"Ah! Glad my memory still works. So, did you do anything fun today?"

"Um, no." She watched the bubbles fizzle in his dark beer. "Nothing too exciting."

He ran a hand through his thinning red hair. "It was a bit dreich out there, wasn't it? Some of my lessons had to be cancelled."

"Lessons?"

"Oh, I work at the outdoor center in the daytime. Have you spent a lot of time down at the loch?"

"Not really." She tried to focus on his pint. But though she wasn't making much eye contact with him, she knew his eyes were fixed on her. Not in an intense, threatening way, but certainly enough to make her feel awkward.

"Well, if you're interested, I do sailing and paddle boat lessons. Archery, too."

"Okay."

"I've loved the outdoors my whole life. I grew up in a city, but my family took all kinds of trips. Lochs, forests, nature reserves."

This reminded Genevieve of her own childhood, especially the boating trips with her dad and brothers. Sometimes her mom would come too, though she usually just complained about the sun being too hot, the boat too fast, they hadn't brought enough snacks. Her dad, as was his way, would just listen and take it in stride.

Both were gone now. Gone forever. She was technically an orphan. That was strange to think about. Even though her dad had been gone for over twenty years, it may as well have been a week ago. Genevieve pushed these thoughts away. She didn't need to feel that grief.

"Are you all right?" Gordon asked, leaning in just enough to be intimate but not intrusive.

"Yes." The dark feeling was still there, but she would plow through it. Distract herself, maybe. Fortunately, the smiling man across from her seemed more than happy to provide distraction. "So, all that, and you're a bartender. Impressive."

"Aye, well, I help Mara in the evenings. In exchange she lets me live here."

"You live in the pub?"

"Upstairs. I'm only here in the summers. Rest of the year I live up in Aviemore, about an hour away."

At that moment, Genevieve realized that Mara was watching them from the bar. Far away as she was, her gaze was too close for comfort. Genevieve averted her eyes, focusing back on Gordon's now slightly emptier pint. "That's nice of her," she muttered.

"She's a good woman. Can be a little scary at first. But she has a lot of heart."

Genevieve made herself smile. Maybe Mara had heart, but not for her. She could still feel that prickly stare. "Janet said the same thing."

"Janet, aye." He lowered his voice. "From what I hear those two used to have a bit of a thing."

"Really?" This was a genuine surprise. But then she remembered how Janet had looked when talking about Mara. Perhaps it wasn't too surprising after all.

"Aye, it was before my time of course." He leaned forward and lowered his voice even more, at this point it resembled a soft squeal. "I suspect Mara and George might have had a thing, too. But of course, that's their business. I shouldn't gossip." Leaning back with a grin, he spoke normally again. "That's my Aunt Gillian coming out."

"And does she have a thing with you?" Genevieve didn't know why she asked this. It wasn't like her to ask something so personal. Maybe she would have back in her "Gen" days, but not now. "Sorry."

Gordon only laughed. "Oh no. No, no, no. She reminds me of my Mum. I think she feels the same way, like I'm the son she never had. Though for all I know, she *does* have a son. Nobody really knows about her life before she came here. Anyway, enough of that."

He went on to tell her stories about his life. Why he moved north from Edinburgh, how he fell in love with the loch and town during a trip while he was in university. How he had studied to be a doctor, but decided that wasn't the life for him, and how, even with all the beautiful lochs and forests in the country, this one was still his favorite. He hoped to build a house in Fonniskie one day. He told her about his brother and two sisters, about his parents, about his grandparents. He spoke of them with such enthusiasm and love. Genevieve found, oddly, that she enjoyed listening to him, just as she loved listening to Janet. He had a youthful vigor, joy, and a passion for the things he spoke about that couldn't be faked.

All the while, Mara continued to stare in their direction.

"Anyway," he said, "I must be boring you."

"No, you're okay." Then, she realized that the pub was empty besides herself, Gordon, and Mara. Dread crept into her again. A question popped into her head, and she felt confident she could trust his answer. "Listen, were you at the outdoor center today?"

"Aye."

"Was there a man there today? Skinny, black hair, named Murdock."

Though unsurprised, she still felt a little sick when he frowned and shook his head. "Not that I know."

She described her encounter with Murdock, just as she had with Janet. If nothing else, it felt good to share.

"That's really weird," Gordon said when she finished. "If there had been a boat accident today, I would've heard about it."

She felt even queasier. "Does he sound like anyone you might know?"

Gordon shook his head. "I've known a lot of Murdocks to be sure, but none fitting that description. Probably an out-of-towner."

"I know him." Mara's firm voice gave both Genevieve and Gordon a jump. Genevieve hadn't even seen her approach, but now she was looming over them, as if she'd teleported. "It's closing time," she added icily.

"Oh, already?" Gordon chuckled.

"You know him?" Genevieve asked Mara, trying to sound less desperate than she was. All she needed was a little closure on the encounter.

"Aye." Mara didn't look at her, instead focusing on scooping up Genevieve and Gordon's glasses. "I wouldn't worry about him. He was probably drunk, or high. Most likely both."

Gordon shrugged. "Well, I never met the man, but I'd take Mara's word over mine any day."

Saying nothing else, Mara carried the glasses back to the bar. Genevieve noticed the light, soundless trot to her step.

"I suppose you best be heading back," Gordon said.

Genevieve nodded. It was a short walk, but Mara's little explanation did nothing to ease the knots in her stomach. It felt like there was something Mara hadn't mentioned.

Apparently, she failed to hide her distress, as Gordon pursed his lips sympathetically. "Would you like me to walk you back?"

Genevieve's stomach let up slightly. As much as she wanted to be proud and say 'no,' she couldn't. "Yes, if it's no trouble."

Her hands were raw and tender after helping Janet pull weeds in the back garden all morning. It hadn't been Genevieve's idea of a fun activity, but she'd felt guilty seeing the older woman alone on her knees out there. Of course, unlike Genevieve, Janet hardly had any trouble doing the work, not even breaking a sweat. Genevieve had to admire the woman's stamina.

After they finished their work and ate lunch, Genevieve felt tired but in high spirits. Even her back was mercifully quiet after all that, though she was certain the pain would eventually strike with a vengeance.

In general, the day seemed to be looking up. She had slept soundly and dreamlessly the night before, and there were no signs of strange, possibly inebriated men. In fact, she felt so good, she decided to go down to the loch again.

She stood by the water, letting the coolness of the air and the warmth of the sun mix on her skin. Across the loch, distant sailboats slid along the water; she wondered if Gordon was on one of them.

Even in the lurid afternoon light, the loch was a sight to behold. But it still felt like a painting, something intangible that she could appreciate but never connect to. Maybe she just had to accept that.

As time went on, she felt a small stinging sensation along her arms and hands—tiny midges nipping at her. She tried to shake and bat them away, to little effect. Perhaps they were telling her to go back to the house? More likely she was reading too deeply into an annoying little bug's afternoon snack.

The water made soft clopping sounds against the shore below her. She peered into its depths, where beneath the dark surface weeds swayed in a gentle rhythm. The motion was calming, in a strange way. She had to keep herself from being too hypnotized by it, lest she faint and fall into the water. Then she noticed something within the rhythmic weeds. At first it looked like a reflection from the sky. But it became quickly clear that it was *beneath* the water, lurking within the weeds. A tiny white orb. She leaned a little further. What was it? A coin? A pearl? Slowly, that feeling of being watched wrapped its grubby arms around her again.

The weeds violently swayed inwards, as if something was pulling them away. At that moment she realized what the orb was. A shining white eye, staring up at her. She only had a murky picture of what it was attached to: an equine head, algae-smothered and rotting, the skull grinning at her from beneath the shallow water.

Her chest tightened. The horse. It was still there after all. Dead and drowned, taken by the loch. Bile gathered at the back of her throat. It would be too late to look away or cover her eyes. The image was already burned into her.

Then, the creature blinked.

The sound that came out of her mouth was unrecognizable, a guttural groan ripping through her throat. She pivoted and sprinted up the hill, pushing her body harder than she had in decades. When she reached

Janet's front door, she vomited the sandwich she'd had for lunch into the shrubbery.

Before she could compose herself, a spindly hand gripped her shoulder. She jerked violently away, nearly tumbling into the vomit-covered plants.

But it was only Janet, her small eyes wide with shock. "I'm sorry, dear."

Genevieve didn't say anything; she just sighed, catching her breath and letting her fluttering heart settle. Once again, Janet ushered her into the living room, and once again, fixed them both some tea.

"What's the matter?" the old woman asked, sitting next to Genevieve. There was genuine care in her voice, a motherly concern that calmed Genevieve's nerves. She wanted to tell Janet everything, but was hardly even sure what had happened. Maybe she only thought she had seen a horse. Her brain took a bunch of vague, underwater flora and shaped an image from it. Or perhaps she actually *had* seen the dead animal. But her mind, or the light, played tricks on her, making her think it blinked.

"I'm fine." The part of her that wanted to tell the truth protested, but there was little point. It was clear now that the loch wasn't the place for her to be. Everything seemed mostly fine when she kept her distance from it. Besides, this was her second to last full day in Fonniskie—then she would never have to see it again.

And if she was indeed losing her mind, at least she could deal with it at home.

"Are you sure?" Janet asked.

"I think I just overexerted myself a little today."

Two more days. Two more days.

"Oh no! I didn't work you too hard this morning, did I?"

Genevieve gave a smile. "No, I enjoyed it." She was pleased to find that she meant that.

CHAPTER FIVE

"Are you all right?"

Genevieve was listlessly watching the green hills and trees roll by her window. The voice pulled her from this trance. "Uh, yeah."

"You've just been a bit quiet," Gordon said, sipping a can of Irn-Bru soda.

"I'm sorry."

"Oh no bother, just wanted to make sure you're fine."

He stopped talking for a bit, letting the only sound be the low rumble of his car against the road. But it wasn't long before he broke the silence and began talking about the different trips he'd taken with his family.

Genevieve sank back into her trance. This was all a bit surreal. Here she was, riding in the car of a man she only met a couple days ago. But she wasn't anxious about that. Everything in the moment seemed distant to her. She hardly even had a feel for what country she was in. The A9 could have just as easily been I-80.

It was hard to say how she even ended up here. The night before she had gone back to the Wet Hoof, almost without a thought. The pub had become a sort of comfort zone, especially after what she had seen in the loch that day.

Strangely, Mara had been more attentive toward Genevieve throughout the evening. Not friendly, just attentive. She asked Genevieve how much longer she was staying in Fonniskie, and what she had planned. Then she asked if Genevieve had been to Loch Ness.

"No, I don't really have that in my agenda." She hadn't mentioned her disinterest in seeing any more lochs.

"It's beautiful this time of year, isn't it Gordon?" Mara asked him.

"Aye, though it's been a while."

"You have the day off tomorrow, don't you?" She patted his shoulder tenderly. "Do you have any plans?"

"Well, not really but ... "

"Why don't you take Genevieve up to Loch Ness, show her Urquhart Castle?" She turned to Genevieve. "You would like that, wouldn't you? Gordon is a terrific tour guide."

"Well ... " As much as she wanted to say no, it was hard to when trapped by those eyes.

"It's almost a two-hour drive," Gordon said with twitches of eagerness in his face, showing that he'd be interested only if Genevieve wanted to do it.

Genevieve had thought about it, though probably not as long as she'd wanted. Ultimately, she had decided it might be fun to get out of town for a while.

Now here she was. Gordon had picked her up after breakfast, which she quickly realized would be the second-to-last breakfast with Janet. That thought made her a little sad. But there was no point in thinking about that, she had a castle to visit. It was funny, when she used to imagine her big Scotland trip, she pictured many castle tours. But this was actually the only one she would be seeing.

Gordon talked almost nonstop the entire way. Sometimes he would ask her questions about herself. Short as her answers were, they gave Gordon more than enough to go off of. When he asked her what she did for a living and she told him, he went on about his cousin who did marketing for a university in Leeds. When he asked if she was married—and she had very little to say on that—he had a lot to say about the fact that he'd never been married. All that time he spoke vivaciously, with that toothy grin on his face. It almost seemed like he was excited to spend time with her. Maybe he even was, but she couldn't imagine why. She wondered if he had a crush on her, even though she was nearly old enough to be his mother. She hoped that wasn't the case. Or, if it was, that he wouldn't try to take it any further.

What also confused her was why Mara cared so much whether or not she saw Urquhart Castle or Loch Ness. Maybe the woman wanted to get her out of town for the day. But why? Something about this situation almost felt like she was going to get driven to the middle of nowhere and murdered. Yet she doubted Gordon would ever hurt anyone. In his rambles, he even reiterated how he liked just about every outdoor activity except hunting.

This was all strange, but she was just going to have to try and enjoy herself.

They reached Loch Ness around noon. It had been cloudy but dry back in Fonniskie, but here there was a light misting. Fortunately, Genevieve had made sure to bring an extra jacket.

She was surprised on learning they would have to pay to see the castle. Mara hadn't mentioned that detail. Fortunately, Gordon happily paid admission for them both. They walked the grounds toward the castle, which looked like a mass of cragged rocks at this point. There seemed to be quite a few people there. Many families with little children. Genevieve was again reminded of her childhood vacations—with the parents who were no longer here. As they walked, Gordon went on about whatever history of the place he could remember. Hundreds and hundreds of years of history.

This would be the oldest architecture Genevieve had ever encountered, by a long shot.

"Want me to take your photo?" he asked, when they came across an old wooden trebuchet on display, standing tall and proud.

"What's that?"

"Your photo. By the trebuchet." His face was puffed up and excited.

"What? Oh no." She hadn't even taken any photos on this trip. There didn't seem to be much point. Who would she even show them to? She certainly didn't want any photos of herself. She couldn't even stand looking in the mirror unless she had to.

"Are you sure?"

Well. It would be something. A record to prove that she'd taken the time to come here, to this other part of the world. Though she was hardly sure what that record was worth. She handed him her phone and stood awkwardly by the trebuchet, giving her best smile.

"Perfect," Gordon said.

When he showed her the photos, she was revolted. Who was this pale thin woman with the greying brown hair? This person, small and frail underneath the large weapon, shoulders hunched and lousy back bowed. Where did she come from? She didn't look like her mother, who had lived a full life—or her father, who hadn't. She looked like a spindly conglomeration of the two, all the unwanted parts conjoined into a sad specimen. Who was that joyless grin for? What were those dull eyes looking at? The woman in the picture looked like a shell—past her prime, just like the trebuchet and the castle. But at least the other two were interesting to look at.

Yet all Gordon said was, "Looks good!"

She tried to imagine what he saw when he looked at her. Apparently, he didn't see what she did. Janet didn't seem to, either. Perhaps nobody else did. Well, maybe Mara did.

"Thanks," she said, resisting the urge to delete the pictures he'd taken. Perhaps she would, at some point.

They walked across a bridge into the castle proper. Most of the building was gone, just stony foundations. Gordon said that it had been destroyed in the late seventeenth century. That was disturbing for her to think about. What a long time to be wrecked, abandoned, all but forgotten. Even though it was an inanimate structure, she felt sorry for it. In fact, all she felt walking through these ruins was sadness and loneliness.

But she kept it together, listening flatly to Gordon, occasionally replying to his statements with an "I see" or an "Oh wow".

By the end of their tour, they were on an overlook, where she could see the long, watery stretch that was Loch Ness. For whatever reason, this loch gave her more peace than the one at Fonniskie. But as she took in the expanse—sitting as it had for centuries and hopefully would for centuries more—that empty, tight feeling pressed harder. Everything around her felt miles away. It was just her and the cragged stranger in those photos.

She tried to push this veil away. To keep it together just a little longer. She even closed her eyes and tried her breathing exercise. It didn't work. Soon the loneliness clutched at her throat and her face grew hot, tears rolling down her cheeks.

"Are you all right?" Gordon asked once again. He leaned in close but didn't touch her.

"Yes." She wiped her face with her hands and tried to push the feeling down again, as hard as she could. "I'm just overwhelmed."

"Aye," Gordon said. "It's quite a sight, isn't it?"

Gordon was relatively quiet during the drive back to Fonniskie. He seemed privy to the fact that Genevieve felt less like conversation than usual. Though the dark feeling inside her faded more by the mile, Genevieve mostly felt numb. In the sky, the clouds were breaking away and slivers of sun were poking through. She couldn't appreciate the sunshine—she'd left her sunglasses back at Janet's house, so the sight was uncomfortably bright. Her back was beginning to ache again, too, as if the pain was gleefully slicing its way into the spotlight. Throughout most of the drive she just closed her eyes and leaned back in her seat.

She most certainly was a "crabbit".

They reached Fonniskie by late afternoon. The ride back had seemed faster than the ride away. The loch shimmered with delight at their arrival.

Genevieve wasn't excited to see it. But what did it matter? She would be leaving tomorrow.

Gordon dropped her off at Janet's house, his face all cheeks, and they exchanged goodbyes. Once she walked up to the front door, she realized she had forgotten to thank him. It was the least she could do after he took time out of his day off to take her on a little excursion that she hadn't really wanted to go on. But when she turned back, his car was already down the street. Maybe he didn't want or need a thank you. But it still made her feel rude. It was doubtful she'd get another chance. She didn't plan on going to the Wet Hoof pub tonight; too tired and sore. All she wanted was take a shower, eat dinner, and slide in to bed. She would pack her things in the morning.

She remembered they'd gotten each other's phone numbers the night before, just in case they needed them during the excursion. A text message. That seemed good enough. Courteous. But writing a decent message would be like composing an email, and she needed that shower first.

The house was quiet when she entered. All the lights were off.

"Janet?"

There was no response. The tireless woman must be out visiting another neighbor. Marching up the stairs, Genevieve fought the urge to go straight into bed and nap. She beelined to the tiny bathroom before she could succumb.

The cold water did its part to zap her awake. She stood under the chilly spray for a long time, eyes closed, hearing the roar of the water against her head, and letting the tired sensation fade away. Then, without notice, an image popped into her mind. A rotting, grinning face beneath the water. Suddenly, the bathroom's musty smell reminded her of aquatic decay, her hair felt like weeds sticking to her body, the water on her skin felt thick and dirty. She finished the rest of her shower quickly.

When she came out of the bathroom, the house was still dark and quiet. Genevieve felt a jab of anxiety.

Was Janet going to come home for dinner? Or was Genevieve going to have to take care of herself tonight? She sighed, ashamed of these anxious thoughts. Janet was a grown woman who could do what she liked and go where she wanted. Genevieve was just a short-term guest, and if she was on her own tonight, then that was that.

She went to her bedroom to dress and compose her message to Gordon. She tried to keep it kind without being too warm. If Gordon indeed had a crush on her, it was best to make her disinterest clear. He was a nice man and perhaps even handsome in his own peculiar way. But she just couldn't even begin to imagine anything with him. Following her long, doomed marriage with Todd, she'd dated a little and had a few one-night stands, but only with men around her own age—older, if anything. And they—well, they weren't terrible people, but they were usually not as friendly or invested as Gordon. She liked it that way.

But perhaps she was just flattering herself. For all she knew, Gordon was as un-attracted to her as she was to him. Maybe even more so. Maybe his kindness just came from pity.

She deleted several drafts before settling on short and simple.

"Gordon, I really appreciate you taking the time to drive me out to see the castle today. That was very kind of you. I hope you take care."

Gordon replied with a smiley face and a beer mug emoji. Perhaps he wasn't quite as verbal in writing. Or maybe she hadn't written the right thing.

She chose not to dwell on the meaning of his response, instead moving on with her evening, checking and writing emails. By 7 p.m., it was very clear that she was on her own. The pang of anxiety came back, and she did her best to fight it away. She wished Janet had at least left a note. But again, she was a grown woman, and so was Genevieve. Janet didn't owe her anything.

She went down to the kitchen and made herself a peanut butter sandwich with some berries on the side. Her last dinner in Fonniskie.

As she ate alone, she heard a faint squeal from outside. Her body went cold. The high-pitched noise sounded similar to a horse. It seemed to come from the back garden. Without a thought, she jumped from her seat and locked both the front and back doors. Janet would be fine; she had her house key with that flashy blue and white lanyard.

Genevieve pushed through her nerves to finish the final remains of her sandwich. As she reached for the last sliver of crust, she heard another squeal. This time, however, it was distinctly the whistling of wind. The day hadn't been too windy, but it must have picked up since she returned to Fonniskie. So, once again it was just her brain playing tricks. She was tired of it.

But no, it wasn't just her. She had to believe that. Something was genuinely wrong in this town. That had been evident since that first morning, even before she saw the black horse. She wasn't going to be sad about leaving Fonniskie.

Well, that wasn't entirely true. She would miss Janet—maybe she would convince the old woman to fly out to her part of the world sometime. Perhaps she would also miss the evenings at the Wet Hoof. They weren't experiences to write home about; all she did there was sit around awkwardly, but it had become a warm and comforting routine. Maybe she would try some bars or pubs in Omaha, see if she could attain the same feeling.

After dinner, she turned on the television in the living room, just for the company. On BBC Scotland, there was a "rewind" program showcasing all the big news stories, music, and events of 1997. There was only one event from that year that encompassed her memory. Her dad's death. It stung her to remember how, before his body was found, it had all seemed like it would be okay. He had acknowledged that he had a problem, that the pills had gone from a necessity after hip surgery to a severe addiction. He had said he would work to get better, had looked her in the eyes and promised that. She'd believed him, believed he would be okay. Then he was found dead in his bedroom, OD'd on a secret stash he had apparently been keeping. Nothing else that year, the next year, or the year after really mattered to her. She had gone through the rest of the '90s in a haze. If the Y2K armageddon had happened, she wouldn't have noticed or minded.

She did eventually start to care again. She moved up in her job and had a marriage to bury. There was, in fact, life after her dad's stupid, senseless, bullshit death.

Still, he should have been here, with her, in this living room, in this house, this town, this country that he had loved his whole life.

She changed the channel to the Scottish parliament, dryly discussing things she didn't really know or care about. She wasn't paying attention anyway, all she wanted was the voices. The room grew darker and her eyes heavier. Janet still wasn't home. She must have been really living it up. Maybe she and Mara were rekindling old sparks. Whatever she was doing, good for her.

When Genevieve couldn't watch any more, she went upstairs, brushed her teeth, changed into her night clothes, and climbed into bed. As she closed her eyes, she heard the front door click open. A wave of relief rushed through her. Janet was home. She wanted to go

Anthony Engebretson

downstairs and say hello, but she was tired and imagined Janet would be too. There was always breakfast.

As she started to drift, a loud clatter from downstairs pulled her back.

"Janet?" she called out. "Are you alright?"

There was no answer. She waited a few moments, holding her breath, listening for any sounds of activity. Her stomach clenched at the long silence. It would be best to check.

She kept calling to Janet as she moved through the hall and down the stairs. When she reached the first floor, she was overwhelmed by a swampy smell. There was a fumbling sound coming from the kitchen. She had the urge to rush back upstairs, grab her phone and call the police. But instead, she let her autopilot guide her into the kitchen. She froze when she saw the dark figure by the fridge, standing amid a cluster of pans, black eyes gazing at her.

"You ... " she said.

Murdock gave her a cold grin.

She slowly stepped backwards, out of the kitchen and toward the front door, trying to control her trembling.

"I want you to come with me," he said, moving toward her, matching each of her steps. He still wore the black raincoat; it was damp as if he had just come in from the rain. He had no shoes or boots, and his pale feet looked strange, bulky, and featureless.

"Where?" she asked, just trying to keep him occupied. Find her moment.

"To the loch," he said, cocking his head as if that were obvious. His grin softened into something almost resembling a compassionate smile. "I know that you'll be happier there."

"Okay."

Murdock offered her his hand. "Shall we?"

"I should get my things."

"You won't need them." There was amusement in his voice, but his face remained soft. "You won't need anything."

Now was the time. She turned toward the front door. But before she could take another step, a strong, slimy hand grabbed her wrist. Murdock pulled her face-to-face with him.

"This is going to be good," he said. His breath smelled like fish, and weeds dangled from his hair. "I can't believe how long I've been waiting."

She tried to pull away from him, but his grip wouldn't give way. It was as if his hand was glued to her wrist. Despite the adrenaline rushing through her body, she felt herself weakening. Her back was beginning to fail her again. Pulling together as much force as she could muster, she kicked him in the shin.

The force hurt her toes, but also seemed to hurt him, and he angrily threw his head back. It did nothing to make him loosen his grip, however. Before Genevieve could make her next move, a long croaking noise came from the bottom of Murdock's throat. His eyes rolled back, turning white, and they seemed to pull apart. His nostrils flattened and enlarged, while his mouth expanded into a grizzly grin. His face pulled away from his head, stretching toward the ceiling. The croaking built up into a throbbing, unearthly scream.

Genevieve wanted to scream, too, but it only came out as a raspy gasp. Her throat had closed up. Her entire body was frozen.

Murdock's bones crackled as his face continued expanding—pine-colored veins pulsing along his growing snout. His ears stretched upwards. At this point, his head resembled that of a dead horse. His hair—now dark green rather than black—flowed down his back like a mane. The swampy odor was more overpowering and suffocating than ever.

He let out another watery, echoey scream, piercing her eardrums. It shot a surge of panic through Genevieve's body. She tugged away as hard as she could, but it felt like trying to pull off her own skin. The pain made her howl, a sound that curdled from the bottom of her throat. Murdock used his other hand to cover her mouth. She felt his slimy palm merge with her lips, and as much as she tried to tug her head away, it was futile. In a desperate move, she kicked his shin again. This time her foot became caught, her toes captured within the slimy skin. She groaned defeatedly. Panic still energized her, especially at the thought of where he was taking her, but the fighting was only hurting her. All she could do was stare up at the long, grotesque face that stared down at her, white eyes gleaming hungrily, mouth twitching with anticipation.

From behind her she heard the door open. "Jesus Fecking Christ!" shouted a voice.

Murdock snorted and squealed in response. Suddenly, Genevieve felt her skin peeling away from his, like a band aid being slowly pulled off. She fell to the ground as the creature retreated into the kitchen. From there came a loud clatter, then silence.

"Are you all right, then?" She looked up and felt a rush of relief to see Gordon's friendly face looking down at her. This time, though, he didn't have his squirrelish smile. His face was drooped, his skin pale, lips trembling and eyes wide.

She wanted to say something, but her voice couldn't muster the strength. It was hard to process what had just happened. She stared again toward the kitchen.

"I think it's gone," Gordon said. To check, he rushed into the kitchen, foolhardily. She thought of Todd. As Gordon rushed off, she stayed on the floor.

Something near her caught her eye. It was a key, attached to a damp white and blue lanyard.

"Fecking Christ!" Gordon shouted, snapping her attention. Her muscles remembered how to work again, and she rose to her feet. As she came into the kitchen, she smelled the outside air and felt wind brushing against her skin. Gordon stood wide-eyed, staring at the jagged entrance where the back door had been.

"We need to call the police," he said, turning to her.

The idea was absurd to Genevieve. What the hell would they do? But if it made Gordon feel better to call them, she wouldn't resist.

After he made the call, they went into the living room to wait. They sat side-by-side on the sofa, Gordon clutching a butcher knife taken from the kitchen.

"What the fuck was that?" he muttered, not for the first time. She never would have thought he had so many expletives in him.

Finally, she felt her voice coming back to her, if lightly, like the feeling in her face coming back after an injection of Novocain. One word came out of her. It sounded silly, absurd, inappropriate. But it was the only word on her mind. "Kelpie."

Gordon scrunched his face and shook his head. But the skepticism in his expression looked weak, unsteady. Then, his eyes widened, and he looked at her as if a revelation had just come to him.

"What?" she said. Her second word. Baby steps.

"I came here to tell you something," he said.

Her first thought was that he was about to confess his love. But by the look in his face, she knew it was something else. Something more serious.

"Janet was found down at the beach tonight," he said. "It must have happened while we were away."

Whatever feeling had returned to Genevieve iced over again. "What?"

Gordon smacked his lips and looked at the floor, trying to find the words. He clutched his knife as if protecting himself from what he needed to say.

"She must have drowned," he said. "She's gone."

CHAPTER SIX

When all was said and done, what choice did she have but to move on?

The police had come, questions were asked, and little came of it. What was to be done with Janet's house was up to her family. How Fonniskie would cope with her loss was up to Fonniskie. What had happened and why, well, Genevieve wouldn't think about that. She'd had a train to Glasgow to catch.

Life would go on. Whatever had happened to her, it would just have to stay where it was. There were bills to pay, work projects to finish, obligations to fulfill.

And life did go on.

The first couple of weeks were hard. Each day it took everything to work up the courage to leave her apartment. She even took some sick days—which was rare, as she never even let the flu stop her from working. Nightmares plagued her, and she had anxiety attacks every time there was a knock on the door. But she pushed herself.

It felt strange to go back to normal, as if she was roleplaying what her life used to be. But she would fake it until she made it. She had to. As the weeks since her time in Fonniskie became months, she grew good at it. There were still the nightmares, and her sleep was terrible. She no longer watched TV after being triggered by the sight of horses in a Western movie one evening.

But there was nothing triggering about work. There were projects to do, and she did them. She took the harsh and witless criticisms of her supervisors and passed that energy down to her own team, from the stern, condescending emails to the awkward meetings, as she was supposed to. Nobody in her office had ever asked about her trip, which was a blessing. The most she ever talked about it was during a phone call with her brother, Andrew. It was just a short chat, a check-in, probably as obligatory for him as it was for her. The call was also the first time she ever talked about Janet's death with someone else. It would probably be the last, too. She didn't want to think about Janet, not ever again.

Her push to force normality seemed to be working. Maybe life would even *feel* normal again in a few months' time. It seemed she was back on the road to contentment. All she ever needed was contentment. It was all she ever asked for.

Then, with several months between her and that awful trip, she received the first email.

It popped into her inbox on a Friday afternoon. The subject caught her attention, as it didn't resemble any other messages she received on her work email:

"COME BACK."

At first, she thought it was spam, and the system had failed to catch it. But then she saw the address it came from, and her heart stopped. It was Janet's.

There was no text in the body in the email, just a link. It was against her nature to click on links attached to strange emails, but this was an exception. The link took her to a day-old article from a news site local to Fonniskie's area. It was the story of a fourteen-year-old girl from Aberdeen who, during a family trip to Fonniskie, had gone missing. After two days, her body had been dredged from the loch.

Genevieve deleted the email and blocked the address. For the first time in a long time, she didn't work at all that weekend. All she could think about was the email. Who had sent it? Was this some sick joke? Something inside of her had a suggestion: *he* had sent it. He had killed the girl.

So, what was his point here? To taunt her? She was safely four thousand miles away from him and his little loch. Whatever happened over there wasn't her problem.

It wasn't.

Once again, life had to go on. Two months went by without any more strange emails. After an incredible chiropractic appointment, her back almost felt normal again. She took up jogging, getting up early every morning. First, she did a light quarter mile, then a half mile, then a full mile. Her pace was light, nothing too straining, she wouldn't push her luck. But it made her feel proud.

Everything was going to be okay. Even her dreams were settling. Or, at least, she was handling them better. The loch, the creature, Janet, the girl—they still found their way in. But at least she always woke up.

Then came the second message. This time it was sent to her personal email.

She received it while having lunch with her co-worker, Angela, who worked in HR. Angela was one of the closest things she had to a "friend", though Genevieve suspected the woman just thirsted for company and settled for whatever she could get. Her phone pinged in the middle of Angela's gabbing about her daughter wasting her life getting a degree in film. Genevieve regretted glancing at the notification. Her stomach clenched when she once again saw Janet's address.

The header this time said, "I DON'T WANT THEM."

Unable to wait until after lunch, she excused herself to the bathroom, shut herself into a stall, took a deep breath, and clicked open the email. It was another empty body, with a link to an article from the same source as the last one. The article was about an elderly man found dead. His body had been near the loch in Fonniskie, of course. The article didn't give many details. Not only had he drowned but he'd also apparently been ravaged by an animal. Authorities and neighbors suspected his own dog might have done it. The animal hadn't been found.

Genevieve felt even sicker when she recognized the man. George, the old man she had encountered that first morning. The man whose dog, she realized, may have saved her then. The quiet man who, those nights at the Wet Hoof, always gave her a nod. Worst of all, his last name was apparently Buchanan—same as hers.

She blocked the email again and spent the rest of lunch in a daze.

That night, she once again lay awake in bed. Why was this all happening? What had she done wrong? Going to Scotland? To a loch that thousands of people visited every year?

What had she ever done to him?

Him. It was strange how easily she accepted what he was. Accepted that she had nearly been killed by a fairytale monster, one that was continuing to torment her, hurting other people in the process.

Amid these rolling thoughts, she recalled a story. It was one of the stories her dad had told her. It was about her great-great-grandfather. Or maybe it went back further than that. He was an ancestor at any rate, and he had lived in Fonniskie. As the story went, a water horse from the loch was causing trouble for the village. It was snatching sheep—she didn't remember seeing any sheep during her time there. One day it decided to go a step further and killed someone's teenaged daughter. Like the girl from Aberdeen. Genevieve's great-great-grandfather or whatever, who was the town blacksmith, devised a plan. He and his son—her great-grandfather perhaps—lured the creature out of the loch with roasted meat. Once they had it vulnerable, they swooped in and jabbed hot, silver hooks into its sides, trapping it. The creature managed to rip away from the hooks and retreat into its watery den, but it never bothered the town again.

Of course, Genevieve had since learned this was a common legend. Though in most versions, the creature ended up dying from the attack, reduced to a pile of jelly the next morning.

But what if, Genevieve thought as the clock turned to 3 a.m., the story was true? So, then his pursuit of her was revenge? Or maybe reparations, her life recompense for the pain her ancestors inflicted on him?

Fuck that. Fuck everything about that. What had happened—if it had even happened—had nothing to do with her. It had even less to do with George or that girl. Or Janet. Genevieve probably had plenty to atone for—she didn't even want to think about it—but not that. Besides, he had caused the people of the village so much pain to make them want to kill him in the first place. Of course, that assumed every detail of that story were true.

Regardless of what had happened, she didn't deserve to die for it.

But would she tell *him* that?

Even after this, she fought tooth and nail to return to life. She jogged, though it became a struggle to go more than half a mile. Focusing on work also became difficult, as hard as she tried—and her mistakes and slips in judgment were earning her nasty emails. One of which, for the first time ever, even called into question the renewal of her yearly contract. But this didn't bother her as much as it should have.

Where she was still capable of paying attention was in her newfound obsession with Kelpie legends. It gave her a sense of comfort to learn all she could. Perhaps it was a sense of control. Few results of her investigation indicated any actual belief that they were real. They were all legends, myths, stories. Still, the stories often lined up with what she experienced—the adhesive skin, the shapeshifting, often taking the form of a normal horse, but sometimes the form of a person. In some places it was suggested they could take the form of other animals at times, like birds. Sometimes the water horse that lived in lochs and seas was considered separate from kelpies, which inhabited rivers and streams. It was called an each-uisge, literally Gaelic for "water horse". Apparently the each-uisge was more vicious and aggressive than the kelpie. But there was debate over whether they were separate creatures or not. She supposed the distinction didn't really matter. Water horse legends weren't just exclusive to Scotland; they had different names and stories throughout Britain, Ireland, and even Scandinavia.

She learned many stories. There was, of course, the one about the butcher, who may or may not have been her great-great-grandfather. Another story was about a kelpie who lured nine children onto its back and pursued a tenth. This last child's hand, or fingers, became stuck to the creature's skin, and the child had to self-mutilate to escape. There was also the legend of the "Laird of Morphie" and the kelpie. In the story, Graham of Morphie, a rich and cruel laird, stole a kelpie's bridle, and wouldn't give it back unless it served him. The horse did hard labor for him for several years, pulling stones up a hill so he could build a castle. Once the castle was finished, the laird gave the kelpie back its bridle, letting it return to where it came from. But the creature was angry and vengeful. It made a promise:

"Sair back and sair banes,

Carryin' the Laird o' Morphie's stanes

The lair o' Morphie'll never thrive

As lang as Kelpie is alive!"

Not long after, the laird, his son, and his wife died, and the castle fell into ruins.

Genevieve doubted there was truth to that one. That version of the creature could be controlled. Also, it was apparently able to place a curse on the entire family, dooming them for all time. They couldn't have truly had that power.

Yet couldn't she also say she was cursed?

One thing the story showed was that these creatures were unforgiving of slights. Whether or not her ancestors had ever slighted him, she certainly had now. Or, at least, that's how he likely perceived it. All she had done was try to live. But she was his chosen prey and from what these stories told her, when these creatures chose their prey, they didn't easily let them go.

Soon enough, she received the next email.

She hardly felt any surprise when she woke from a restless sleep and found it in her inboxes—both her work and personal email. It was from a new address, a slight variation on Janet's regular one.

"COME BACK" was the subject line again. Attached was another article from the same site. People were searching for a young couple from London, missing for several days. Of course, they had been visiting Fonniskie. It didn't mention anything about them being found. Police seemed confident that they were ruling out any foul play—just like they'd "ruled it out" for Janet, George, and the girl. They could only hope that the couple would turn up somewhere and not be another "tragic accident" in what was shaping up to be one rough year for Fonniskie. Genevieve knew that hope was worthless—the couple were either at the bottom of the loch, fish nibbling at their bloated bodies, or they were rotting along the shore somewhere, waiting to be found. Or maybe he had eaten them.

Regardless, they were certainly dead. Five lives taken. More to come. And what could Genevieve do? There was nothing anyone could do.

Well, that wasn't true.

She could go back.

That was what he wanted. Go back to his loch, so he could reach her. It was the course of action that made the most—and the least—sense. She wanted to ignore this. Maybe change her email addresses, change her phone number, move to a different house, town, country, whatever she needed to do. Then maybe one day she could forget him.

But that would never happen. As the days went by, she could hardly eat, or sleep, or think. When she did sleep, the nightmares made her not want to any longer. Her performance at work slipped by the day and her bosses reviled her. It was almost a sure thing that her contract wouldn't be renewed. But she didn't even care about that. He was in her head. He had been worming his way in since that first morning in Fonniskie. She could unplug, throw away her phone and computer, change her name, change her face, quit her job, move to China, Cambodia, Antarctica, or fucking Mars. But no matter where she went or what she did, he would be there, swimming through the contours of her brain, gnawing at its fickle flesh.

She had never felt this way before. Through so much of her life, she was always able to pull away. The creature *had* cursed her, it seemed, and it was one hell of a curse. "Sair back, sair banes." Wherever she went, every face she saw would be the ghost of another life he had taken or was about to take. Every shadow would be his. Every drop of water would be his slimy touch. Nothing would stop him—even if authorities became wise to his existence, he transcended all logic and procedures. They could drain his whole goddamn loch, and he would still find a way.

His curse would eat at her until there was nothing left, and she would crumble and die where she stood. Nobody would help her. Nobody would understand the malignant passenger she carried. She was alone.

There was one option that sometimes popped into her mind. She could end it all. Maybe she could score some opioids, reunite with her dad using the same means he did. She wouldn't be breaking any hearts. Her brothers would be sad for a little while. But they would grieve the girl they knew more than the woman they didn't. Her sisters-in-law and nieces and nephews would have little to miss. Her team despised her. Her employers were probably already looking for someone else; even Angela began to look at her differently. Maybe Todd would find old feelings bubbling up and would break down at the news. More likely, he would just laugh.

But who cared and who didn't wouldn't matter to her. She would have nothing to worry about.

No. She didn't want to die. Something in her wanted to keep going, no matter how painful it was.

So, the only other option that she could possibly fathom at this point was to go back to Scotland. Back to Fonniskie.

Of course, if she did that, she would likely just die anyway.

But maybe not. She could find another way. After all, she had been wrong, she wasn't fully alone. There was one person who knew, who had seen what she had and—as far as she knew—was still alive. Gordon.

But he was there. Everything was there.

So, with the calm resolve of a martyr, she booked her plane tickets and sent an email to her bosses saying she would be out indefinitely due to an emergency. She didn't care how they'd reply. The tickets were one way. Whatever else, she would figure it out when she got there.

It wasn't like her to not make any plans. Her first trip to Scotland had been planned a year in advance. But things had made at least a little sense back then.

Only one thing was certain. She was going back to Fonniskie.

CHAPTER SEVEN

Every TSA checkpoint, every dull wait in a terminal, every long flight was just an encore of what she had done nearly a year before. She was in a haze, on autopilot. When all was said and done, it was like she'd taken one step in Omaha's airport and the next in Glasgow's.

It was once she was past Customs when it finally sank in where she was and what she was doing. Dread crept through her body, encompassing her. As her head cleared, her own mortality became tangible again.

Next steps. She took one of those ever-useless deep breaths. All that mattered were next steps. Which were?

She turned on her phone, ignoring the countless email notifications, and called Gordon. To her relief, he answered.

"Genevieve!" he said. No matter how peppy he tried to sound, she could hear the exhaustion in his voice. "How are you doing?"

"I'm in Glasgow," she said.

Gordon's cheery pretense melted away. "Why?"

"Are you in Fonniskie? I can be there tonight."

He sighed, as if she'd said what he feared. "That's not a good idea."

"I know what he's been doing," she said, realizing how tired, practically lifeless, her own voice sounded.

"What, who ..?" It sounded like Gordon was about to try and play dumb, but thought better of it. "It wouldn't be good for you to come here."

"It has to stop."

"We can handle this."

We? Who was *we*? Curious as she was, she didn't ask. She just said, "I'll be there as soon as I can," and hung up. When he tried calling back, she ignored him.

*

It wasn't until the next morning that she finally reached Fonniskie, the loch shimmering in the low morning sun, seemingly excited to see her once again. She wasn't happy to see it. But strangely, now that she was here, her anxiety dissipated.

It could have been in her head, but the town felt emptier than before. There wasn't a soul out on the streets, the houses dark and lifeless. It didn't even look like there were any boats out on the loch.

She had her driver drop her off at the Wet Hoof pub. It was the only place she could think to go. The sight of the old stone building gave her a warm yet melancholic feeling. This had been a place of, maybe not joy, but at least comfort during her time here. There was a loving innocence in its greeting.

Beside the building was another familiar sight: a slender, silver-haired woman staring out at the river. Only after the driver took off did Mara turn and acknowledge Genevieve. Her mouth curved into a smile, her copper eyes gleaming. For whatever reason, this smile was more unnerving than any of her glares.

"Gordon said you'd be coming," she said, looking Genevieve up and down. Genevieve realized how terrible she probably looked. Nor did she even want to imagine how she smelled after two long and sleepless days of planes and trains. "Why don't we go inside?"

Inside, the pub was dark and empty, dust motes floating in the sunlight that reached into the room. The smell of must overpowered any other scent. It was strange to see the Wet Hoof like this, looking and feeling like a mausoleum.

Gordon was sitting by the bar. He glanced up as the two women entered, and frowned. His appearance startled Genevieve—pale, gaunt, unshaven, he looked terminally ill.

"How about a drink?" Mara asked, sliding her way behind the bar. "It'll be on the house, of course. At least the first one." She was excessively perky, as if she had absorbed all the energy from the rest of the room.

"No thank you," said Genevieve.

"Well, at least sit down," she said, patting the counter. "We've much to discuss."

Genevieve did so, climbing onto a stool next to Gordon. She dropped her light backpack on the floor next to her. It held all she had brought this time—a few clothes, some medication, her passport, phone, and money. Most of these she brought just in case there was an "after" to all this.

"Hey Gordon," she said with a quick smile, hoping to pull out some of that old cheer. She didn't get any; he just looked at her and nodded blankly.

"Well," Mara said, pouring herself a glass of scotch, "we have quite a problem, it seems."

"Does she know about it?" Genevieve asked Gordon. The answer, she realized, was probably obvious.

"The kelpie, you mean?" Mara interrupted before he could open his mouth. "Aye, all too well." There was a sad and weary familiarity to her voice.

A twinge of hope flared in Genevieve's gut. "How do we stop him?"

"This isn't your fight," Gordon cut in.

"He's tried to take me," she snapped. Seeing the way Gordon flinched and shrank made her feel guilty, so she softened her tone. "You saw it. Besides, I'm the reason he's doing this. I can't let anyone else die."

"No, you're not," Gordon said, firming himself back up. "You can't possibly blame yourself."

"She's right," Mara said flatly, sloshing her drink about in her glass. "He's always been a wee radge. It's the nature of his kind. But most of the time, he's kept to himself, didn't cause any harm or trouble. You've triggered something in him. I don't know what, but I don't think he'll stop until he has you."

"Or until we kill him," Gordon interjected.

"Aye." Mara sipped her drink.

Genevieve felt sick to her stomach. All of this she already knew, but hearing someone else say it stung.

"Why me?" she asked. To her shame, her voice sounded young and helpless. A young Gen's voice.

Unmoved, Mara simply shrugged. "It doesn't really matter, does it? What matters is how to end this."

Genevieve felt deflated, though she didn't know why. She already had her own theories for why the kelpie was targeting her and wasn't sure what Mara could have contributed to that. But perhaps she'd hoped the woman would give her a little more certainty or insight. Maybe even reveal something to make it all make sense.

"I have it handled," Gordon said.

"Aye right," Mara said sarcastically. "How many nights have you spent freezing your arse off, hunting shadows? Meanwhile he's snatched three people, right under your nose. I've been tellin' you, over and over, to catch this creature, you have to use his own tactics. Lure him. To lure him, you need the right bait." She looked directly at Genevieve.

"You don't mean ..?" Gordon also stared at Genevieve. She hadn't thought his face could become any more flushed, but she'd been wrong. "Christ." He looked back at Mara. "Are you fucking kidding me?"

Mara shrugged.

Genevieve wasn't shocked by the idea. It made sense. Besides, just coming out here, she'd already put herself on a platter for him. Still, she tried not to think about it too deeply, lest it truly sink in.

"We're not using Genevieve as bait!" Gordon said, his voice thick with disgust. "Christ."

"What do you suggest instead?" Mara snapped. "A cooked piece of meat? A sheep? Don't underestimate him. How many times do I have to tell you that, Gordon? He's been around longer than any of us can imagine. He's watched the world change around him and has adapted again and again. But we're lucky. We know one weakness of his." She began pouring herself another glass. "Obsession. Mind-numbing obsession. He can drown and murder as many people as he likes, but there's now only one life that will satisfy him. Maybe you can't see it, and you don't have to. I do." She pointed at Genevieve. "And *she* bloody well can."

Gordon looked helplessly at Genevieve. She gave a reassuring nod, though it didn't seem like he was looking for her confirmation.

"It's not right," Gordon mumbled.

For a moment, Genevieve thought Mara's anger was going to escalate—there was an enraged flash in her eyes. But the flash was brief and immediately melted away, her face softening. "My sweet lad," she said, gently reaching across the counter and placing her hand on Gordon's. "Nothing about this is right, is it?"

"You don't deserve this," he mumbled to Genevieve.

"No, she doesn't," Mara said. Though Genevieve had a hunch she wasn't being completely honest about her feelings on that. "But did George deserve it? Or Janet?" Her voice cracked slightly at the second name. "Did that poor couple deserve it?" She turned to Genevieve. "They found one of the bodies yesterday. Haven't yet identified which." She focused back on Gordon. "That girl? My god, did she deserve it? Not to mention whoever might be next if we don't put an end to this. Who deserves this, Gordon? Tell me."

He didn't say anything. He just frowned, staring at Mara's smooth hand resting on top of his.

"But if anyone can kill him," Mara continued, her voice nearly a whisper, "can take the shot that would end him for good, I have faith that it's you. Don't leave Genevieve and me to fend for ourselves." Genevieve wondered how Mara could be so certain about all this. What kind of history did she have with that creature?

Gordon only frowned more deeply. He pulled his hand away from Mara's, gently prying her skin off his. "I need a drink," he said.

Mara smiled and pulled another glass from the shelf.

"So, what do we do first?" said Genevieve.

"First? You're going to go upstairs and bathe," said Mara, filling Gordon's glass. "Then get some rest. You look and smell like shite, if I can be so blunt. We can make a plan tomorrow."

Mara's comments made Genevieve realize just how exhausted she was. Her body felt drained, her head murky. Her back was also beginning to flare up.

"You get some sleep, too," Mara said to Gordon, pushing his glass to him.

Gordon clutched his drink and shook his head. "It's not safe."

"He won't come here." There wasn't an ounce of doubt in Mara's voice. "We're too close to the river. The loch's his domain; he doesn't go near the river."

"How do you know?" said Gordon, something Genevieve herself wanted to ask.

Mara clicked her tongue. "If you don't trust me by now, you never will."

Exhausted as she was, Genevieve also wasn't reassured. "Is there even time to rest?"

Mara glared at Genevieve, apparently out of patience. "If you want any chance of surviving this," she said, "then make damn sure you're well rested."

The blaring morning light forced her out of bed. For a minute, looking at the compact bedroom around her, she nearly forgot where she was. This calm, dazed ignorance only lasted a moment. But when it all came back to her, she didn't feel fear. If anything, there was only a gentle hum of dread in the back of her mind. She had enjoyed the best sleep in a long time. And she could only remember one dream. It hadn't been a nightmare, just a dream. It didn't have anything to do with lochs, or drowning, or death. It had nothing to do with *him*. It. That thing.

No, in this dream, she had been free.

She had been in a forest, hiking a nameless but familiar trail with her dad. It had been the version of him that she'd constructed in girlhood—that impervious, restless man who ran on a special fuel, always having the next adventure planned and the drive to start it *right away*. The man who didn't exist—a character, just like she had molded her mother into a warm, loving automaton with little ambition outside of the unconditional joy her children brought her.

Both characters had vanished as Genevieve became older, exposing the flawed, complicated, and, at times, disappointing people they really were. Or maybe even those had simply been new characters. Maybe she never truly knew anybody; everyone, as she knew them, was simply a character of her own design. Her parents, her coworkers, her brothers, Todd. What would her life had been if she'd truly known the people they were rather than creating her own versions of them.

Would such a thing have even been possible? And what character was Genevieve? She tried to construct an icy, though friendly when appropriate, straight-to-business archetype for herself and the people around her. But if she spent her life seeing others as characters of her own perception, then perhaps they did the same for her, and all her efforts to create that persona had been meaningless.

What character had the man in her dream, marching up that mysterious trail without breaking a sweat, seen in her? They had said nothing to each other. The forest had been silent all around them, the trail stretching endlessly. She had known that, beyond them, the world was changing, warping itself into something unrecognizable. But at least the forest would always be the same. At the end of her dream, her father had turned and smiled at her.

"Shake a leg," he'd said.

Then she had woken up.

If that would be the last dream of her life, she wouldn't complain.

She changed out of her night-time clothes, perhaps for the last time, into a shirt and jeans. In the hallway, she found Gordon sitting along the wall like a sentry, rifle against his chest. He looked like he was asleep, or at the very least pondering something, but as soon as she stepped out of the room, he peered up alertly. His face was dull, so weary. He was far from the bubbly, carefree character he had once been—or that she had constructed him as.

"Morning," he said.

"Have you been out here all night?"

He shrugged. "Felt safer," he said, glancing towards the stairs.

She nodded, trying to look as understanding as she could. "Have you slept at all?"

"A little."

She leaned against the wall across from him and stared at his rifle. It looked old.

Noticing her staring, he clutched the gun. "I know how to use this well enough," he said defensively. "I've always had a good eye. I taught archery at the center, mind. Oh, and I'm licensed, so don't worry."

Genevieve smiled. "I'm American. I could buy one of those at Wal-Mart."

Gordon nodded, not smiling back. "Aye, well, it's a pain in the arse here." She noticed he was trembling.

She felt like she needed to comfort him, reassure him. But she didn't know how. "But Mara told me that the most effective way to kill that thing is with hot silver. She already had the rounds and the gun."

"Silver bullets?" She remembered seeing some things about silver when reading about the each-uisge.

"Like werewolves," said Gordon. To her pleasant surprise, a shadow of a smile jerked at the corner of his mouth.

She looked up and down the hallway, the only doors belonging to the guest room where she had slept, Gordon's room, and the bathroom. "Where does Mara sleep?"

Gordon shrugged. "Somewhere downstairs. I've never really seen where she sleeps, to be honest."

Genevieve nodded. If anyone had done a good job molding a character for themselves—a hard, intimidating, but supposedly big-hearted woman—and imposing it on the world, or at least on Genevieve, it was Mara. "How does she know about him? The creature, I mean."

Gordon shook his head. "She never told me. But she does know quite a bit, doesn't she?"

She had to swallow an involuntarily pang of irritation. In the little time she knew him, Gordon had asked her everything about herself. Yet, when it came to the woman who was "like a mother" to him, he didn't even seem curious.

"You want some breakfast?" he asked.

"Yes." To her surprise, she *was* hungry. In fact, she wanted a big breakfast; something like the one Janet had made for her that first morning.

Just down the stairs was a kitchen, cozy and homey. One could easily forget there was an entire pub in the room next to it.

Genevieve didn't end up having the big breakfast she'd craved, just some coffee, buttered toast and a few slices of bacon. But she was content. She and Gordon ate in silence, he holding his gun the way she used to hold her Eeyore doll when she was a small girl. But she had held her little donkey close during mealtimes to protect him. Gordon's intention with the gun was the opposite.

The meal was surprisingly pleasant—the sunlight filling the room, the smell of coffee and bacon blending nostalgically. It was a comfort to have Gordon's presence near her, even as sad and quiet as he had become. It took her back to those meals with Janet, where she had felt close to connecting with someone.

But the warm atmosphere froze over the moment Mara trotted into the room.

"You want breakfast?" Gordon asked her.

"Already ate," she replied. "Let's make our plan."

CHAPTER EIGHT

The black water lapped at the rocky shore, reaching for her. Every *plop* sent a tiny jolt through her body. The world was calm, brightened by the full moonlight. Mara had been correct, this was the perfect night—it gave them the most visibility. As much as something in her wanted to call it off, to retreat, to try again tomorrow, she stayed in her spot. It had to be tonight. She tried to keep her mind blank. All it would take was one doubt to make her lose her nerve completely. Even now, sitting there, watching the silver loch that leered back at her, she was tiptoeing over a precipice. If she slipped, it would be impossible not to retreat. As she watched the restless water, she fought away the image of being pulled into its cold, black depths.

She looked to her right, where a clump of trees swayed in the freezing wind. Gordon was there, somewhere, watching and waiting, rifle at the ready. She trusted that he was alert. But what if his aim wasn't as good as he thought? Or the moonlight wasn't bright enough? Or the gun jammed?

These were just more thoughts that needed to be pushed away. She couldn't let herself believe that the most likely outcome was her death.

She shivered. Her entire body seemed to be telling her to change course. Her back ached, her bones tingled.

"Sair back, sair banes."

The wait went on and on. She caught herself chewing her fingernails, a nervous habit she hadn't indulged in since college. Each moment, she expected to see the creature's head—whatever form it took—rising from the water. But there was nothing. He had to know she was there; he had to see her or at least smell her. What was he waiting for? Was he torturing her with the wait because she had made *him* wait? Maybe it was some weird power move. Like at work, when she would have meetings with her supervisor that he would be fifteen minutes late to, giving her no choice but to wait and perhaps let her guard down. Fortunately, she'd gotten good at not letting her guard down. Whatever game this was, she was determined to win.

She blew on her numb fingers, fighting to grip the hilt of the knife Gordon had given her. It was more for a symbolic sense of security than anything. The blade wasn't hot, nor was it silver. Mara said piercing the kelpie's skin would be like trying to cut a loaf of French bread with a butter knife. Her best bet, as Mara suggested, would be to aim for his eyes. But even if she hit a bullseye—right through his iris—there was no guarantee it would be fatal. And if he survived, it would hardly be a major loss for him, even if she took out both eyes. He knew the loch and the world around it so well that sight was practically a formality at this point. But he would most certainly be pissed.

If nothing else, though, the knife made her feel better, more empowered.

Genevieve still wondered how Mara knew so much about the creature. Why wasn't she out here, helping them? It couldn't have been her age. She seemed unusually youthful and spry for however old she was supposed to be. She also had plenty to say on the matter.

"Be careful," the woman had gravely told them, but more specifically, to Gordon. "Be smart."

The waiting went on, and on, and on. It took Genevieve back to school, when she would stare at the clock, waiting for it to hit 3:30; then the bell would ring and she'd be free for the day. Enough of this bullshit. She wanted to shout out to the fucker, tell him she was here. Tell him to grow some balls and get her. But her voice didn't have the energy.

Maybe he wanted to make her feel alone. Mission accomplished. The feeling wasn't new, but sitting in the dark and the cold, the dimly lit mounds that were the town of Fonniskie far on the other side of the loch, the outdoor center and its beach quietly in her periphery, it was more pronounced than ever.

Perhaps she had been born with this aloneness. Even in high school, when she had been surrounded by people—as a top student, volleyball player, track player, president of the FBLA—she was still alone. In college, her social life seemingly took off. But the friends she had made then, she'd long lost contact with. She'd started dating Todd then, too. Fourteen years of marriage never made her feel less alone. If anything, it made it worse.

The only person she ever had any real connection to had been her dad. But she suspected that was because he had felt as alone as her. A man who loved adventure, but chose to settle for a family life, an accountant at a respectable firm; a man who loved his wife and children but had few close friends and rarely got along with his neighbors. Perhaps he and Genevieve were bonded by the aloneness.

She shook away the reflection and rumination, realizing that, in a way, her life was flashing before her eyes. It didn't need to. Her life didn't have to end here. They had a plan. Gordon was alert and ready, and she believed his aim would be true.

If he was even there.

No, he was. And he was determined. If he didn't feel confident in his aim, he would come rushing out of those trees, telling her they would have to try again tomorrow. She trusted he would. Every situation had its what-ifs. There was always the chance of things going wrong. She would accept that. That was the point of trust.

A dark shape appeared on the moonlit water, floating toward her. Her heart stopped. Here he was. It was time.

But the shape neither looked like a horse, nor a pale young man. At first it was hard to tell *what* it looked like. A piece of floating debris? Then she recognized the boat shape of its body, a thin neck stretching toward a flat beak. Some type of large bird. She couldn't tell if it was a swan, a goose, an abnormally large duck. She breathed again, partially relieved but also disappointed that the wait had to continue.

The bird floated closer. She felt it watching her and a chill crept down her aching spine. Something was wrong here, but she wasn't sure what. Her impulses brought her to her stinging feet, turning to the trees where Gordon waited. She pulled herself together to stop from taking another step; to turn and face the loch again. The bird stopped its approach, cocking its head toward the trees as well. It looked for a long time, as if considering something. It glanced back at Genevieve. From where she stood, the eyes seemed strange.

Like two pale orbs.

Hot panic rushed through her chest. She stepped backward, stumbling and slipping on the rocks and crashing onto her bottom. No time to feel the pain, she scrambled back to her feet. The bird was moving again, but not toward her—toward the trees. Toward Gordon. Once it was close to the shore, it leapt—not flew, but leapt— into the trees.

Everything went silent. Even the wind and the water eased their movement, stopping to wait and listen. When Genevieve felt herself regaining her senses, she knew she needed to do something, anything.

When a sound cut through the silence, she knew it was too late. The sound, a piercing scream, vibrated her blood. The trees began to shake and crack. Then something burst through them—a shadowy mass, tangled in weeds and algae. The mass galloped toward the loch, and at the tip of its tail was a pale screaming head. Gordon, stuck helplessly to the tangled mass. It leapt into the water, barely leaving a splash. The screaming was snuffed out.

Then it was just Genevieve, the loch, and the moon. *Oh God.*

She wanted to throw up. What had just happened? It seemed like there was something she needed to be doing, but she didn't know what. Was she supposed to leap in there after them? Or maybe she was supposed to run to the trees, see if Gordon had dropped the gun. If he had, then she could finish the job. Turning and running away—that was what she wanted to do more than anything, but it seemed like the last thing she should do. What was right? What was the choice that would end this, here and now?

And Gordon. Oh God, Gordon.

The dark mass rose from the water, like a log that had been long submerged. At the head of the mass, she saw the two orbs again, now fixed entirely on her.

She didn't think any more. She ran up the trail she and Gordon had come from, letting the moonlight guide her way. Behind her, she felt the shape following—heard the breathing, snorting, the dense thudding of hooves. She could smell its swampy stench. Not once did she think to glance back. She wouldn't dare. No thoughts spun through her head now, only the drive to keep going—stick to the trail. If she moved any other direction in this wild maze, she would lose her bearings, unable to recognize left from right. Then he would have her.

A dark structure appeared ahead of her. The outdoor center. Gordon's bright green car waited in the parking lot. She paused, realizing that she didn't have the keys. Gordon did. Or he had. She hissed angrily, but there wasn't time to stew. Behind her, the trees crackled, and from the corner of her eye she saw the mass approaching, its pace a sluggish trot. She could feel the white eyes, gawking at her through damp moss.

There was no choice but to run again. She had paused long enough to notice that her chest was burning, her legs were beginning to wobble, her throat was dry and her back gave its stinging cries. But she couldn't listen to it, not right now. She ran toward the road. It was good that she had taken up jogging recently or her body never would have pulled this off.

Behind her, she still heard the clopping and snorting. It was getting closer, and she was getting slower. Her body was failing her. She could almost feel the massive teeth gnashing at her hair, the creature's breath an acidic mix of hot and cold. At any moment, her skin would snap against his, and he would drag her to her into the loch. She wouldn't even be able to cut herself away, self-mutilate for a quick escape; she had dropped her knife.

With an angry scream, she pushed harder.

Then, the clopping ceased, as did the snorting and breathing. The last thing she heard was a shrill, echoey squeal. When she finally stopped, gasping for air, feeling as if her heart was about to explode, she looked back to see that the mass was gone. Perhaps she had gotten far enough from the loch; maybe he couldn't go any further. Once again, she was alone with the empty road and the dark hills and trees around her. But she didn't feel any relief. She was exhausted, her body in agony.

And they'd failed. Gordon was gone.

Her stomach tightened to the point where she bent over and vomited onto the pavement, spewing up her dinner from earlier—a quiet, somber little meal of French fries—or "chips"—and sandwiches that she and Gordon had shared together. They had both eaten in silence, an air of terror and hope between them. Now he was dead, and her stomach was empty.

All there was to do now was limp back to Fonniskie. She didn't want to think about having to tell Mara what had happened. The loss was awful enough. In fact, she didn't want to think about anything right now, except for each painful step.

CHAPTER NINE

The pub greeted her lifelessly when she came trudging through its door—the lights were dim, somber. She crawled her aching body onto the nearest seat. Once she caught her breath and let her muscles ease, she noticed Mara, sitting along the bar, sipping a drink.

"Well," the woman said, without turning. From the raw tone of her voice, it seemed like she already knew what had happened.

Genevieve opened her mouth to respond, but her dry throat couldn't release the words. She closed her eyes, taking in the warmth of the room. When she opened them again, Mara was staring at her, eyes tense like a predator focusing on its prey, her long face scrunched in what looked like a mixture of disgust and despair.

"I told you to be smart." Something about Mara's voice seemed different. It seemed as if her accent was being slowly eaten away by a flat, robotic cadence. "Why didn't you listen to me?"

"We—we … " Genevieve still couldn't form words. What could she even say?

Mara slid from her seat and slowly approached Genevieve. Whatever shoes she wore, the dull sound they made against the floor rang through the room. "I always had a bad feeling about you—stuffy American bitch who hardly even knew why she was here. Hardly even *wanted* to be here. I'm not wrong, am I? And look at what you've caused."

A darkness filled the room, a hateful and evil shadow. Mara was the epicenter. Genevieve felt the need to run again. Unfortunately, there was no more running left in her.

"Now, even Gordon … " Mara stopped moving and swallowed whatever feeling was arising. "You were supposed to end this," she said, when only her hatred remained again. "You started it after all."

There was a weak flare of anger in Genevieve's chest. What had she done to start this? But as badly as she wanted to say something, the words wouldn't come. She was so tired, and her throat was parched; she needed water.

"You thought you could just go back to your miserable life?" Mara said. She began moving toward Genevieve again, each clopping step pounding like a hammer. "Forget all this while people are dying and suffering? No, that wouldn't be right, would it? That's why I brought you back here."

"You." At first Genevieve was confused. How had Mara brought her back here? Then the realization hit her. "You sent those emails?"

A smile crept across Mara's face. The malicious curve her mouth made was worse than any hateful look she could give. "I had to lure you back somehow. In your profession, you should understand how important it is to know the best bait for your prey."

Mara stopped moving once again, as now she was close as she could be to Genevieve, towering over her, eclipsing the light of the room. Genevieve turned away; the musty smell permeating the pub seemed to come from Mara.

"Truth be told, I wasn't sure if I could appeal to your compassion," the woman said. "But I knew I could appeal to your fear. Haunt you the way he did." She let out a cold laugh. "Oh my, you didn't really think *he* would ever know how to use a computer, did you?"

Genevieve turned her eyes further from Mara's, looking to the floor. But when she saw Mara's feet, she felt sick. They were bare and filthy, mossy and gangrenous, covered in light green veins—and she didn't have any toes, just two fleshy masses beneath distorted, curved heels. The masses were stout and bell-shaped. They almost looked like ...

Genevieve looked back up at Mara's face. This time, she recognized something in the woman's face that she'd never noticed before. The features were perfect, symmetrical, broken only by a few strategic wrinkles. In those golden eyes was a familiar, hungry stare. All Genevieve could see in that face was Murdock.

A surge of panic went through her, and she scrambled out of her seat. Mara grabbed her wrist, the same way he had.

"Now then," Mara said, her voice even more robotic. "Relax."

Genevieve tried to tug away but couldn't escape. She realized with horror that the skin of her wrist was fused to Mara's palm.

"Look at me," Mara hissed. She pulled Genevieve to her, bringing them face to face. Genevieve had no choice but to look into those eyes, which seemed darker than before. "I'm not him. Okay?"

The panic still coursed through Genevieve's body, but she was oddly still now, hardly even trembling. It was as if Mara's gaze had paralyzed her.

"Okay?" Mara demanded.

Genevieve gave a dumbstruck nod. She didn't know why she believed Mara. There was no reason to trust this monster. But if there was any point left in resisting, she couldn't see it. There was a strange sensation on the skin of her wrist, the stinging of a band aid being pulled off, and Mara released her.

"So," Mara, or whatever the hell she was, said, "you need a drink."

Without taking an answer, she trotted to the bar. "I'm sorry you had to see them," she said, fixing a drink while Genevieve stood paralyzed, contemplating whether to stay or run. "My hooves, I mean. I know they're not the prettiest sight. But it's hard to maintain every part all the time. At one point or another, you must let loose, you know?"

Mara's tone had relaxed, but the bitter hatred was still there. Though at least the spite gave flavor to her otherwise soulless voice.

Genevieve's mind still raced, but before she could make any kind of decision, Mara was standing before her, handing her a glass of water. Though unsure if she could trust it, Genevieve's thirst was so overwhelming that she didn't care. She greedily downed the whole glass, the cool water flowing down her throat. There was a slightly dirty aftertaste to it, but it was otherwise bliss. The whole time, Mara quietly watched her, unsmiling. It could have been in Genevieve's head, but the woman's eyes seemed further apart, her face longer.

"You'll have to pay if you want another one," Mara said, sitting at the table next to them and motioning for Genevieve to do the same. With the flick of Mara's thin wrist, she obeyed.

"You trust me, then? Good. If I'd been him, do you think I would waste my time with this runabout? I'd drag you to the loch and be done with it."

"But you are ..?" Genevieve couldn't find the words.

Mara found them for her. "A water horse? Each-uisge? Kelpie? Nuggle? Whatever the bloody hell you want to call us? Sure. But I'm nothing like him. First of all, my home is the river. His is the loch."

"You ... " Genevieve had so many questions, yet none at all.

"I tried, you know. I tried to keep you away from him, and him from you." The memory of the trip to Loch Ness that Mara had been so insistent about popped into Genevieve's mind. It made sense now. "I even tried to speak to him, convince him to stop this foolishness." Mara looked at her hands, curling the fingers in and out—as if admiring her work. A dark, disgusted look came over her face. "He wouldn't listen. The damn fool has never listened to me. Honestly, I don't know what he saw in you." She inhaled deeply through her nose. "Or smelled in you."

"My ancestor," Genevieve muttered, thinking out loud.

"Pardon?"

Genevieve told Mara the story of her ancestor, the kelpie, the searing hot silver hooks. A part of her hoped that Mara would be familiar with that story, could confirm it. The smile that spread across Mara's face made that hope grow. "I see."

"Is that story true then?" Genevieve asked, unsuccessfully trying to sound indifferent.

Mara only shrugged. "It doesn't matter if it's true or not. Maybe he smelled some dead old butcher on you. Maybe you reminded him of someone he knew long ago—another woman who had been the ... subject of his obsession. Or perhaps your misery just appealed to him. Or he just couldn't take the loneliness anymore, and you were just the first poor soul that caught his attention." The playful smile faded from Mara's face. "It is a lonely life. Fish are no good company. You can't even imagine, centuries lurking alone in your home, watching them on the surface. Sometimes you come up to be among them; to play with them, or seduce them, or kill them. But you are never *of* them. Sometimes, they even hurt you. Now, he and I had each other, to an extent but ... Well, we are territorial creatures, each with our own precious realm to keep. He's my kin, but not my friend."

There was a glassy look in those golden eyes. It almost looked as though Mara was going to cry. Genevieve had a sudden thought that she was supposed to reach over and touch her hand. But she had no desire to. Mara had made their relationship clear; they owed each other no sympathy.

"I've lived a long time," Mara reflected, the tears never coming. "I don't even know how long. Much of my past feels like a dream. I can remember when there was a Pictish village here." In her voice, there seemed to be uncertainty as to whether that was true or not. "So many years watching history go by, watching people love, fuck, die. I wanted to be a part of it. So badly. And one day ... " She motioned to the pub around her. "I made my move. I made these people *my* people. I was finally *of* them. I couldn't have imagined how special these past years would be. I've made friends. Oh, and enemies, ha!" She paused, her eyes glistening with a youthful bliss that Genevieve couldn't help but envy. "I've fallen in love."

But her eyes just as quickly darkened, and she frowned. "But *he* never could have made the choice I did. It's not in him. He hates humans, you may have guessed. But at the same time, I know he feels that same emptiness, maybe even more deeply than I ever did."

The frown contorted into a scowl, and the bright, reminiscent gaze was completely gone. Once again, nothing remained but contempt. "For whatever reason, he chose you. Marked you. I thought it would end once you left, but the bloodlust you caused ... "

A little bit of Genevieve's energy had returned, and she wasn't going to take that again. "It's not my fault," she snapped.

"He wanted you," Mara bit back. "One sad, joyless woman to fill the darkness in him. He killed Janet just so he could get you alone, you know that? And when he couldn't have you, the bastard tried to fill the void with innocents."

This hit Genevieve hard, but she fought through it. "That's *his* fault ... "

Mara's glare became incandescent, forcing Genevieve into silence. "They're my people. *Mine*! Janet, Gordon, George. The bloody bastard took them from me, and all he wants is *you*."

Despite the glare, Genevieve found her footing again. "Why didn't *you* do anything then? Why didn't you deal with him? Instead, you had to drag me back here ... "

"He wants *you*."

"But why didn't you do anything about it?" Genevieve was losing control of herself. It was like those heated fights with Todd, when she would take off like a sailboat in the wind once the argument really got going. "Why did Gordon and I have to go out there alone?"

"The loch is his domain," she said. "The river is mine."

"What the fuck does that even mean?"

Now Mara seemed taken aback, the flame in her eyes fading. "You wouldn't understand."

"Are you weaker than him?"

"There are things that you ... "

"Or are you just afraid of him?"

Mara leapt to her feet. The sound that came from her mouth was inhuman—a high, watery squeal. The sailboat crashed, and Genevieve was again silent. But she pushed through the fear, staring back at Mara firmly.

"I think," Mara said, calming herself, "I should have just tied you up and left you at the river's mouth for him. Maybe I still should." Genevieve clenched her fists, trying not to let her fear take control. If Mara decided to attack, she didn't know if she could fight back. Fortunately, from the shrug she gave, the silver-haired woman seemed uninterested in this plan. "But at this point, I wouldn't mind seeing the bastard die either."

Saying nothing else, Mara turned and trotted off, disappearing through a door behind the bar, leaving Genevieve alone. The air returned to the room, but Genevieve still felt overwhelmed with hopelessness and despair. She had no idea what to do at this point. What were her options? Despite everything, she still didn't want to die. If she had, it would have made everything so much easier.

Deep down she knew there was no other choice. She was going to have to go back to the loch and face him. Yet strangely enough—and it could have been the exhaustion—she didn't feel afraid.

Mara galloped back into the room. Her skin seemed more sickly and greenish than before, her face longer, her hair akin to a mane. In one hand she held a sharp, rusty object. For a moment, Genevieve thought she was going to attack with it and flinched. But instead, Mara just dropped it onto the table. It was an old, rusty hook—only a few patches on it still shined, gleaming brightly as silver.

"The eyes," Mara said. "Aim for the eyes."

Genevieve picked up the hook, cold and heavy in her hands. She wanted to argue, to resist, to demand a different plan, demand that *Mara* do something. But the fact was, she'd made her choice the minute she booked a last-minute flight to Glasgow again. She was in this to the end.

"Just finish it," Mara said. "I don't care if he dies, or if you do. Frankly, I would prefer the both of you rot in hell."

The sun was just beginning to rise when she left the Wet Hoof pub, like a billowing red flame on the horizon. The loch reflected its glow, looking like a massive pool of lava. It beckoned to Genevieve, offering warmth in the cold.

This time, she followed its call.

Her feet were as sore as the rest of her body, as well as blistered. But none of that mattered. Every painful sting, every cramp, every tremble felt distant. She sucked in the cold air, clutching the hook tightly, and moved onward through the silent town. It wasn't long before she was in front of the little blue, triangular house that had taken her in many months ago. Now it was empty, devoid of the warmth, light and love that had once been there; that she herself had felt.

Down the hill from her and this now-loveless tomb was the loch, and standing before it, watching her, was a thin, pale man in a black raincoat.

It was time.

She kept her eyes on him as she moved down the hill, nearly slipping on the grass. She watched those sharp dark eyes as closely as they watched her back. He was smiling at her. It was a cruel smile, but not cruel just for the sake of it. There was more there than just malice; there was kindness—though a kindness born of desire and hunger.

But there was even more than that, something deeper behind those dark eyes, that fragile smile. She saw fear. It was a fear she was too familiar with—not the kind that he'd made her feel these past months, that was gone now—this was an older, fathomless fear.

This feeling united them, a thread that pulled them together. And she wouldn't push away, not anymore.

Hiding the hook behind her back, Genevieve paused only inches from the figure. He offered his hand. No, not a hand; it was a veined, fleshy hoof, like Mara's feet had been. But Genevieve didn't flinch at the sight. With her free hand, she reached out, even though her muscles tightened as if trying to warn her away. She paid this no mind; this was something that needed to be done. And even as her fingers grasped the slimy hoof, her skin beginning to fuse to his, all fear was fading away.

The creature scowled, closing his eyes and shuddering uncomfortably.

"It's okay," Genevieve said, and she meant it.

It took him some time, but he finally relaxed, the discomfort melting away. He smiled again, basking in her touch. "Thank you."

In the end, after all the bloodshed and murder and horror he had unleashed since she came to Fonniskie, this was all he wanted, to hold her, to enrapture her. To consume her.

His eyes flew open and began pulling apart from each other. Bones crackled as his nose flattened, and his mouth stretched outward, the corners breaking into a grin. His raincoat warped and tightened, taking on the color and greasy texture of his skin, which had once again turned a sickly green. Along his ribs, dark scars revealed themselves, as if tearing their way into existence.

The hoof Genevieve gripped took on the color of black mold. This mildew seemed to spread to her own skin, climbing up her hand and arm, making them appear frostbit. Bursts of panic went through her body, but she didn't entertain them. Hours ago, she would have been overcome by fear, but now she welcomed it. She welcomed the powerlessness. The more comfortable he was—the more he felt safe, secure, in control—the best chance she had.

Besides, though she had no control, she also felt safe and secure. It was a warm and sheltering feeling, like being in a mother's womb. But she tried to keep her distance from it. If she gave in, that would be the end.

The creature let out a watery whinny and pulled her to him, clutching her against his chest. At first the feeling against her cheek was cold and wet. But as she felt her cheek fuse into his skin, the warmth became even deeper. The pain in her body faded away. The creature let out a gentle sigh, his warm breath coursing through her hair.

It became harder to fight the urge to submit. As she melted into him, all of the burden, responsibility and agony of life was vanishing. She didn't want to lose this feeling.

But still, she wanted to live. She didn't want it to end this way, no matter how good it felt. This bastard didn't get to decide how her life ended. He'd made that choice for too many people. She couldn't forget them—Janet, Gordon, George, that girl, that couple—she should have learned all their names. But she wouldn't forget their fear. When this thing took them, had it felt warm and safe? No, more likely it had been cold, paralyzing, a burning agony as their lungs filled with water.

It wouldn't be fair to let it end like this. It wouldn't be just. Not for them.

Not for her either.

Letting this resolve give her strength, she raised the hook with her free hand. It was impossible to see, but she felt sure she was aiming at the right place. Once she was fully confident in her aim, she pressed tighter against him, keeping her free arm from touching his skin, and swung the hook forward.

It felt like cutting into a thick piece of meat, but the hook went deep. As soon as she heard the squelch, she knew her target had been hit. The hook was in his eye. The creature let out a high squeal that the entire town was certain to hear. The noise gave her a melancholic satisfaction. The creature thrashed them both about as he continued crying in pain.

Then, she felt her feet lift into the air. They were falling forward. She still couldn't see anything but knew what was happening. The creature was descending into the loch and taking her with him. The cold water pierced her skin, snatching away every warm and safe sensation. Fear and something else rushed back through her body—the will to live.

She pulled and tugged, trying to escape as they descended deeper into the dark waters, but his skin stubbornly held her. The creature still slowly jerked and thrashed, battling the pain. His guttural cries guzzled through the water. Genevieve realized that she was screaming, too.

But she didn't stop fighting. Little by little, she felt her skin breaking away from his. There was hope. There was a chance, even as the cold darkness completely took her.

CHAPTER TEN

The loch was asleep.

Perhaps it would never wake up. Its waters were still, comatose, as if they had been painted into the landscape. She watched them for a long time, her hooves planted firmly in the dirt, waiting for some kind of life. A simple fish if nothing else. But there was nothing.

She stood along the river's mouth, as close to the loch as she ever dared go. The loch had always been forbidden to her, poisonous. Just as the river had been to him. The idea of dipping even a minuscule part of her body in those waters was mortifying. It felt as if the act would evaporate her on the spot. Certainly, it would be a violation of their ancient kinship. Not to mention an act of violence. An invasion. Besides, she liked the river better. It was freer, took her farther—even then, she had always felt compelled to stay near the loch. Why that was, she might never know.

Maybe it was because of him. There had been a time, she could remember, when she'd thought he was all she had. Then she'd realized that she could be human, could choose to live among them while he chose to be a monster.

But a disturbing question crossed her mind lately. What if he had been right all along? Here she was, her and her river, alone under the cold morning sky. Not human, but in her equine form, which was far more comfortable, more natural. The sun was there but offered no warmth, no company. And the loch—the wild, dangerous loch—couldn't even open its eyes.

She snorted angrily and stamped her hoof, as if that would awaken the dormant waters. Perhaps it had worked, because moments later, something floated from the loch and onto the riverbank. It looked like some of the water had clumped together and congealed. Jelly. It was him, or what was left of him. Her kin, floating carelessly close to the river, closer than he ever dared in life. He was invading her space, violating their code, because nothing mattered to him any longer.

Her fury was dizzying. She hadn't thought she could despise him any more than she already did, and certainly not now that he was dead. Raising her head, she squealed into the air. The noise seemed to reach the whole world. She would have feared it awakening the village, but to her, everything was empty: Fonniskie, the river, the loch. She was alone. She hated him so much, him and that pathetic American he had hungered for.

But the sting of seeing him in this state—reduced to sludge, floating away from his beloved loch—was something other than hatred. This she knew. She looked out at the horizon, wondering how many of their kind were left. In an age where faeries and spirits were so rare, where humans and their systems held temporary power, and they distorted and deformed the land to their own liking—it seemed likely that she was alone.

It just didn't make sense. Why couldn't he have adapted as she had? He could have found the beauty in humans, the community among them. All he would have needed to do was try. His ways had always been a mystery to her. It was why, above any other feelings, she had feared him.

But there was nothing to fear now. The American had ended him. She peered intently at the loch, seeing if she could catch any sign of the woman. Even if it was just a shapeless mass, bobbing along the surface. But she saw nothing. Hopefully Genevieve was dead. It was unjust that she would live when so many—Janet, Gordon—didn't. Genevieve was an empty woman. Mara had recognized that the moment she saw her. That emptiness had filled the room, demanding Mara's attention like an old friend coming to visit. But now Genevieve was gone. Alive or dead, she was part of the loch now, entwined with it. This gave Mara an odd pang of jealousy.

She turned away; she'd had enough and headed back toward her river, to its quiet flow. The sight aroused no warmth or comfort, as much as she reached for those feelings. She looked to the large stone building, the establishment she had made her own, had gone to great lengths to make a reality. It seemed like an antique now; a dead, decaying castle. She rotated back to the river, galloping into the water. This was one last desperate measure, one last attempt to feel.

After submerging her entire body underneath the surface, she contorted into her truest form. Her body bulleted against the current, bestriding the rocks, the grass and algae. Fish brushed against her body. She breathed the water, which nourished her more than oxygen.

But even as she became part of the river, she felt simply like a passenger, watching blankly as she was steered into the murk and the darkness.

CONTENT WARNING

Drug overdose, parent death, child death, suicidal ideation.

ACKNOWLEDGEMENTS

I want to thank my fiancée, Taylor, for supporting me in this and all things. I also want to thank my parents, JS and Alec, for always being reliable and helpful beta readers.

Thank you as well to my writing group, particularly Dylan Relue, Anush Balayan, Colin Mack and Alison Turchi for their invaluable critiques and feedback that helped me make this novella the best it can be.

Writing a story set in a country I have never been to (yet) was a unique challenge for me. The town of Fonniskie, its loch, and river are entirely my invention, but I based them loosely on the real world village of Kincraig and the neighboring Loch Insh and River Spey. Many sources online helped paint a picture of life in Scotland for me, as well as the folklore of the kelpie. I won't be able to list every source, but I would like to give shout outs in particular to the Youtube channels Shaun (Vlogger), BeautyCreep and WeeScottishLass, and podcasts Stories of Scotland and Fabulous

Folklore with Icy. It has been fun to learn about such a fascinating (and magical) country, I hope my depiction in this book has done it some justice. I can't wait to go there soon.

Thank you to Antonia and Ghost Orchid Press for giving my book a chance and sharing it with the world. It has been a true pleasure to work with them on this, and I hope I can collaborate with them again soon.

Lastly I want to thank everyone who reads this book, reviews it, buys it, rents it, borrows it, and/or plugs it. Thank you as well to all the friends and family who haven't been named, for loving me and believing in me. Your support, whatever form it takes, means the world to me.

Anthony Engebretson
2022

ABOUT THE AUTHOR

Anthony Engebretson lives in Lincoln, Nebraska with his cat, Cicero. He has been published in several anthologies including Cloaked Press's *Spring Into SciFi 2018* and *Spring Into SciFi 2019*, the Writer's Coop's *The Rabbit Hole Volume 1*, and Martinus Publishing's *Forbidden: Tales of Repression, Restriction, & Rebellion.* He was also co-editor of the anthology *Prolescaryet: Tales of Horror and Class Warfare.* His long-suffering blog is at raccoonalleyblog.wordpress.com.

Made in United States
North Haven, CT
12 May 2022

19117945R00100